CORNERED!

Trevannon palmed open the door and stepped into the murky hallway. He instantly froze as the bobbing flare of a lantern appeared in the stairwell, filling the corridor with its diffused glare. Trevannon's hand brushed his holster, reaching for the gun Treat had taken, before he remembered. He stopped dead, facing the stone-faced giant coming up the stairs with a lantern in one hamlike fist, a leveled gun in the other. Jans Vandermeer had caught up at last. And crowding behind the sheriff's bulk was the grinning face of Bill Treat. . . .

D0963285

RAMROD RIDER

by T. V. Olsen

FAWCETT GOLD MEDAL • NEW YORK

A Fawcett Gold Medal Book
Published by Ballantine Books
Copyright © 1961 by Fawcett Publications, Inc.

ISBN 0-449-13080-0

Manufactured in the United States of America

First Fawcett Gold Medal Edition: March 1974
First Ballantine Books Edition: December 1986

CHAPTER 1

A GRAY, STEADY RAIN FELL FAR INTO THE MORNING. IT streamed in silvery torrents off rocks and ledges, and lashed a tight grove of young aspen which stood like glistening specters beyond the cave mouth. Standing under a granite overhang which shelved the low entrance, Wes Trevannon thought, *This is the day for sure.*

He leaned a shoulder against the rock, hands jammed in his pockets, a tall and big-boned man of thirty-five. Broad in no part of his body, he wore soft faded denims which emphasized an all-over rawhide leanness. His bony face was long and somber, not quite homely. His sun-bleached yellow hair was shaggy and untrimmed, eyes deep-set and of a slatey off-gray, eyes that held a sort of alert and positive self-certainty mingled with an indifferent cynicism. When a gust of wind-lashed rain matted his hair against his bare head, he shook himself and turned back into the cave which briefly bisected a steep hillside.

Two horses were hobbled at the rear of the cave. Trevannon's own sugans were neatly rolled and lay by his saddle; on the other side of the dead fire, Cal Kittredge snored on in his blankets. Trevannon went to him, bent and shook him by the shoulder.

Kittredge groaned and sat blearily upright. Ran his long pale hands over dark thinning hair and yawned. He was a slight and graying man of fifty whose once fine and aquiline features were mercilessly highlighted by the dead-gray

1

daylight, showing deeply incised lines of dissipation, folds of slack flesh below the chin. He started to speak, this single effort setting off a violent fit of coughing. He reached beneath his blankets and drew out a square flask. Uncapped it and pulled deeply.

Trevannon watched this familiar ritual with a neutral patience. He said with no reproof, "Better wait till after."

Kittredge lowered the flask. Ruddy fever spots glowed in his sallow cheeks. "You're right." He grinned. "Some medicine, though." His hand dipped into a waistcoat pocket of his shabby, sleep-wrinkled black suit, and drew out a gold watch on a tarnished chain. "Ten to eight, eh?" He heaved to his feet and hobbled in his sock feet to the cave mouth, squinting out at the dreary morning. "By God. This'll be it. Our day, man. When did it start?"

"Storm broke about midnight. Slackened off some now, but it's holding steady."

"Perfect so far. Now if the bank opens punctually at eight . . ."

Travannon nodded. "Let's get started."

He went to a rock shelf running along the cave wall, lifted down twin bundles, and tossed one to Kittredge. No words were necessary, for they had rehearsed the details two days ago. The bundles contained identical patched and well-worn slickers, battered hats, run-down half boots, and faded red bandannas. When each had donned his outfit, they made two anonymously similar figures, the long, shapeless slickers concealing them from neck to boot-tops, except that Trevannon was a head taller. They saddled their horses, packed on their gear and rode out from the cave, immediately swinging southeast.

They rode steadily for a quarter of an hour, crossing a range of brush-clogged hills hazily cloaked in the smoky downpour of rain. They descended the steep switchbacks of a final slope and rode down into the town of Cedar Wells.

Collars turned high and hats tugged low, the slicker-shrouded pair headed down the sweep of rain-pocked mud that was the main street. Misty rows of ramshackle false fronts flanked its wagon-channeled length. Trevannon gave the first building, a fairly new brick structure, a brief attention because it housed the sheriff's office.

His straight mouth formed a smile. *Square under the nose of that damned Dutchman,* he thought, with no personal malice to it. He knew of Sheriff Jans Vandermeer only what he'd heard, and that was enough. Covering this great, sprawling New Mexico county of his jurisdiction, with its broken wilderness and mountain terrain, was no cinch, but Vandermeer, with his handful of deputies, was said to do so with dogged efficiency.

Trevannon had dryly observed as much to Cal Kittredge when the consumptive little gambler had approached him with the scheme. Kittredge dealt faro at the Lucky Angel Casino and daily banked the house winnings. Fall round-up on this plateau range was over, and the cattle buyers had already left, leaving the town bank bulging with the local cattlemen's cash proceeds. Kittredge had taken careful note of the bank safe. A ponderous, old-fashioned affair, ill-suited to handle the flush of prosperity the local ranches had suddenly known after many lean years . . . a few good ones had added up to a small fortune in that battered old safe.

Cal Kittredge meant to take it. But he needed a companion who could handle trouble. He watched the men who came and went. Chose Wes Trevannon, an out-at-the-heels drifter with a ready-worn gun, who came in one night for a quiet game. Kittredge had played as he'd never played, till Trevannon's small stack of chips was heaped at his own elbow. Then he'd leaned across the table.

"Trying to build up your stake, eh, friend?"

"Was," Trevannon said dryly.

"No offense, but you're puny odds in this game. Just now I'm thinking of another kind. Something in your looks says that you're the man I want." He'd paused deliberately. "Run to the law with it, and I'll name you a liar."

"What law?" Trevannon had murmured, and then: "I'm listening."

When Kittredge had outlined the job, Trevannon voiced his doubts—first, about going up against the iron-stubborn tenacity of a sheriff whom lawbreakers might outwit for a time but could rarely lose. Secondly, about the slim chances of only two men pulling a daylight holdup. Kittredge had the answer: the rainy fall weather was moving in. He, Kittredge, would quit his job here, buy up food supplies, and pack them up to a cave he had found a mile north of town. Later Trevannon would join him. So far as the townsfolk would know, both would have ridden on separately.

They would set up camp and wait for a day of bad weather, when few or no citizens would be stirring abroad in Cedar Wells. Even on ordinary days, the bank's business was generally poor for an hour after it opened. Heavy rain would minimize the likelihood of interruption during the few minutes they'd need, would help them pass unnoticed in and out of town, and would quickly obliterate their trail. Even Jans Vandermeer would be baffled, especially if they swiftly lost themselves in the brushy hills above Cedar Wells. They would line out in a due southerly route toward Mexico; in a few days they'd be well beyond Cedar Wells County and its dogged sheriff. . . .

Trevannon felt the cold fist of tension close around his guts as they cantered diagonally across to the bank tie rail midway down the street. Swinging down, he fought back the feeling, looped his reins around the crosspole.

Standing by their horses, the two men swiftly opened their slickers enough to be able to reach their guns easily. They drew up their bandannas to cover noses and mouths. Kittredge ducked beneath the tie rail and crossed the rain-slick sidewalk to the bank entrance, Trevannon at his heels. They palmed out their guns as they went through the double doors.

A young clerk stood behind the half-partition that enclosed his cage, leaning his elbows on his window counter, his thin, precise mouth touched by a smile at something the other clerk had said. He casually turned his head as the doors opened, then his tall thin body froze and his smile went wooden. The other was a slight, gray-haired man who was sweeping the floor, his back to them. He turned with gouty unhaste at the other's sudden silence. "Dave, what the—" The old man broke off, seeing the masks and guns, let the broom clatter to the floor as he raised his hands.

Kittredge crossed the room and thrust his gun across the counter. "Open the safe. Fast and no tricks. Fill that, large bills only—I'll be watching." He shoved a grain sack under the bars.

The young clerk stood dumbfounded. His mouth worked a little, like a fish's out of water.

"Fast, I said!"

The clerk did move then, scurrying down on his knees by the bulky old safe. His thin fingers twirled the dial. Trevannon had remained by the door, dividing his attention between the street outside and the elderly clerk, who hadn't stirred a muscle.

Kittredge shifted his feet, the creak of a floorboard very loud in a stillness broken only by the blind ticking of the square-faced wall clock. He snapped, "Shag into it."

"Missed a turn," the young clerk whispered, not looking up. His sweating brow gleamed palely.

Wes felt a nervous pulse begin its drumroll against his temples; he could only guess at Kittredge's state of mind. But the combination was suddenly completed; the cashier turned the handle. The door swung wide. A grate of steel on steel as a drawer was pulled out, and another. The slicker was a roasting, air-tight confinement, and sweat drops broke out on Trevannon's face and ran in a stinging wash into his eyes. He blinked them away.

The clerk held up the bulging sack. Kittredge said, "On your feet and bring it over. Do it slowly. . . ."

The clerk carefully obeyed, sliding the bag across the counter. Kittredge blindly snatched it up and swung for the doors. At once the clerk's hand slashed down beneath the counter, came up with a small-caliber pistol. Trevannon's gun lifted chest-high and he shot. The clerk gave a howl of pain. Kittredge pivoted back as the young man slumped across the counter, clutching his arm.

Kittredge started to bring up his gun; Trevannon stepped forward and batted his arm down. "That shot'll bring half the town," he grated. "Come on—move!"

He sprinted out the door with Kittredge at his heels. They were on their horses and reining about within seconds, but already Trevannon was dimly aware of shouting men pouring from doorways along the street. Trevannon raked the flanks of his bright bay gelding, and Kittredge numbly followed his lead. They lined out down the street at a hard run, leaning low in their saddles. Some fugitive shots bellowed in their wake as one or two armed townsmen rallied enough to open up.

They reached street's end and careened their horses around the last building, cutting off from the street. Wes reined aside to let Kittredge take the lead, and the gambler blindly spurred his horse into a heavy thicket. Branches backlashed wetly against their faces and bodies. Kittredge burst through onto a grassy slope and spurred savagely to its crest. Trevannon was directly behind as they rode down the other side into a timbered vale, and then he hauled up beside Kittredge and grasped his reins, bringing him to a halt.

"Let go, you damned fool!"

Trevannon's acid speech ate coldly into the man's terror. "Get a hold on yourself! Said you had a route figured out that'd take us up into the back country off the beaten way. You're running blind—get on it!"

Kittredge rubbed a shaky palm over his wet face. "Sorry. Yes. All right. We strike up south along that hogback ridge." He pointed. "It'll take us five miles away from town and we'll never hit a road or a house."

Fifteen minutes later they were riding the summit of the long ridge. They would have been skylined here, save for the thick pine cover; needle-fall made a springy carpet that left no sign beneath their horses' hoofs. Kittredge breathed easier, now free of his clutching panic that had almost wrecked the operation.

He said mildly, "I owe you a vote of thanks. Lost my head."

"Damnfool thing, turning your back on a man you just robbed."

"I was lucky. You were there. Paid your way for sure."

The grain sack slung from his saddlehorn brushed Kittredge's knee; he reached down and touched its papery contents with a soft, sly smile. Trevannon had seen the smile before; it had come to him strongly that Cal Kittredge was no man to trust—a consideration which hadn't worried him then. But now they were two men alone with a grain sack containing a small fortune, and Kittredge no longer needed him.

The thin smile held on Kittredge's face as he studied Trevannon's impassive one. "Man, no wonder you didn't do well at faro; you're a poker player."

"But I don't gamble with stakes this high," Trevannon said softly, flatly. "Don't fall behind me, Cal."

Kittredge chuckled; it set off a retching spasm of coughing that doubled his frail frame. He straightened, gasping for breath. He nodded at the old game trail that followed the ridge summit, winding between two pine boles. "Well, it's a fine broad patch . . . and I've no particular disposition to trust you either, m'lad. We'll ride abreast."

Together they gigged their animals into motion, watching one another from the tails of their eyes. Trevannon observed narrowly that the trail just ahead began to pinch down; a bit farther, a huge pine grew from its center, dividing it. His muscles pulled tense as he neck-reined his mount toward the right to pass on that side of the pine. As the tree's bulk passed between them, he dropped his hand to brush back his slicker skirt and expose his holstered gun.

Even so, the quickness of Kittredge's maneuver caught him by surprise. In the brief instant that the treetrunk concealed him, Kittredge magically produced a gun. As their horses moved past the tree, the little weapon barked in his fist. Trevannon was already half-twisted in the saddle to face his companion, at the same time lifting his Colt from leather, when the gambler fired. Wes felt the wrenching blow in his side. Then the Colt came up in a tight arc and bellowed close to his body, beneath his half-raised left arm.

Kittredge's body rose and tilted sidelong. A thin hand fumbled at his pommel in a dying effort to brace himself. He coughed once and rolled slackly from his saddle. His horse bolted and dragged its rider, foot hung in the stirrup, a half dozen yards before pulling to a halt.

Trevannon sheathed his gun. He looked at Kittredge's still body as it swayed grotesquely to a slight motion of his mount. *He had to have it all. The poor bastard. He had to have all the money, and it got rougher'n ever he dreamed.*

CHAPTER 2

He STEADIED HIS FIDDLE-FOOTING ANIMAL BEFORE DIS-
mounting to check his wound. He stripped off his slicker,
tattered denim jacket, and calico shirt, and dropped them to
the ground. He had to crane his head over his shoulder to
see where the bullet had entered; it had cut cleanly through
the fleshy part high in his left underarm. Kittredge had shot
point-blank but hastily; the hurt was not serious, though
bleeding copiously from back and front. As the numbness
of the bullet's impact receded, the wound burned like fire.

Trevannon unknotted his neckerchief and, catching an
end in his teeth, passed it around the triceps muscle tight
against the wound, tied it tightly. He didn't judge the hurt
grave enough to cause immediate concern, though it needed
better attention.

Aware of the wet chill biting to his bones, Wes quickly
picked up his clothes and shrugged gingerly into them. He
tramped over to Kittredge's horse and it shied away, skittish
with the smell of blood. He quieted it with a hand on the
reins and the good quiet words that men use to animals.
Loosened Kittredge's hung-up foot from the stirrup and let it
thud soddenly to the ground. Threw the worn saddle gear
off the horse and cut it across the rump with the bridle. It
bolted back down the trail.

Trevannon knelt by Kittredge to search his clothing. The
gun caught his eye—a silver-mounted English pocket pistol

that hugged the dead man's wrist, concealed by the sleeve, held there by a slender length of elastic which would stretch with a snap of the forearm, dropping it smoothly into the palm. Trevannon's lips tightened as he went through the pockets. There was only the watch, a fine, well-worn piece with an inscription on its inner case: *To Calvin on His Sixteenth Birthday, from Father;* and a flat wallet containing, except for a few silver dollars, only an old and faded daguerreotype of a young and sweet-faced girl.

For a moment Trevannon pondered over these slender tokens of a gentle upbringing that yet summed up a wasted lifetime. Then, decisively, returned them to the dead man's pockets. He gathered up the body and carried it into a deep thicket, laid it out on the bare ground in an awkward semblance of sleeping dignity. He returned for the saddle and bridle and left these by the corpse. To dig a permanent grave and rock-shore it against scavengers would take hours; he had neither the time nor the strength for the job. The brief exertion blazed abrupt pain into his wound, which had settled to a throbbing ache.

He returned to his horse carrying the sack of money, looped it over the horn. Stood a moment with an arm slung across the saddle swell, thinking. . . . Sheriff Vandermeer would be especially incensed by this daylight holdup pulled nearly under his nose, and wouldn't rest till he'd found the men. That meant, Trevannon thought, that he must waste no time in getting beyond the range of posses, holding the while to deep cover away from roads and human habitations. And he was handicapped, as Vandermeer was not, by his ignorance of this country to which his scattered driftings hadn't previously taken him.

He had depended on asking directions of Kittredge before they parted. During idle talks in their cave, the gambler had mentioned only that the ridge tapered off five miles south. What lay beyond, Wes had no inkling. Still, the ridge would take him that much farther from Cedar Wells; then he'd play the tune by ear. They had covered perhaps a mile when

Kittredge had made his treacherous move. Trevannon wondered whether the shots might have been heard by a tracking posse; Jans Vandermeer would be swiftly on the trail, and no telling how far or near he was at this moment. . . .

The thought galvanized him to movement. He toed into the stirrup, swung stiffly astride, and kicked the bay gelding forward. His animal was unusually big and rangy, long-legged and sound of wind, a stayer. That much was in his favor. In a chase he should hold an easy lead on his pursuers.

Riding the game path between the monotonous walls of dark, flanking pines, Wes Trevannon's mind was drained to numb tiredness by the flurry of violence; his thoughts drifted.

Lucy, Lucy, if you had only lived. . . . That's right, Trevannon, make her your excuse; blame the dead. All right, all right; it wasn't just Lucy or the boy dying, there were plenty of other things. . . .

When had he really stopped giving a damn? A ranch, a wife, a son, self-respect. A poor man slaved for years, drove himself on a shoestring and a dream, to win such things. Then one by one the shorings of his life were stripped away. First four bloody years of war that shattered a man's ideals and human illusions. Returning to Texas to find his wife and five-year-old son living in poverty, his cattle running wild with no market in prospect. Two years of barest existence. Mortgaging finally to the hilt for the means to round up his wild longhorns and drive them north to Abilene, booming new railroad mecca for the impoverished Texas cattlemen. Two weeks later seeing his herd, dead and dying of Texas Fever, strewn for miles along the banks of the Red River. Returning home in the wake of a sudden typhus epidemic to find his son dead, his wife nearly gone.

Remember the good we had together, Wes. Forget the rest. Almost Lucy's last words, those. Only later, when grief had dulled, had he realized how she'd been telling him to draw strength from that part of memory which framed their life together, the strength that he would need alone. And he'd failed. . . . Self-respect was the last mooring he'd lost, and to his shame it had been easily swept away.

First the penny-ante brand-blotting to restock his range. Soon irate neighbors had come with the law; he'd cleared out ahead of them. Threw in with a wild bunch of ex-jayhawkers who were raiding the northbound trail herds. Quick, crooked money, quickly thrown away in company with trigger-wild companions . . . hard-drinking nights and bloody brawls in the wide-open Kansas trail towns. Always in the background the hurts he wanted to forget, till he was past caring even of forgetfulness. And the driftings, always aimless, to keep ahead of the memories you couldn't outride.

Odd though; all those other things, the brand-blotting, the rustling, brawlings and shootings, had been wild and spontaneous, part of a savage outpour of grief. Years had passed since he had buried his family. Strangely, when he'd ridden into Cedar Wells a couple of days ago, it was as though the blunted edge of that grief, his very indifference, had been in itself a healing, or a start of healing. He had been obscurely and drunkenly toying with that thought over his cards and whiskey when Kittredge had announced his plan. This planned holdup had been his first truly calculated act of crime. Why, if he'd begun to feel his way back to manhood?

Maybe that was it. Maybe he had needed to hit rock-bottom before he was ripe for a change. That, Wes realized wryly, didn't make sense; but neither did this sudden keen and lifting exultance in him, in spite of the danger he faced. An hour ago he hadn't cared whether he lived or died. Now he wanted to taste what life held next. It was as though in casting over the past, worrying out each dreary fact, he'd opened a sore and flushed it clean.

A half-hour later he left the ridge at its southern off-tapering tip and continued to push blindly south, aligning landmarks to hold a straight route. No other way to get direction, but it made for long delays, pushing through alternate bands of heavy timber and brush that pummeled and punished horse and rider. The rain was increasing again, belching windlashed gust against their leaning bodies. Chill and dampness worked beneath the collar and skirt of Trevannon's slicker till he was drenched and shivering. Impatience drove him like a galling spur.

When he broke from the forest onto a stretch of wagon road that evidently belonged to an outlying ranch, he didn't hesitate to follow its twisting, muddy ribbon southeast. The anvil-blows of thunder mounted with the flicker of lightning, drowning all other sound. And so he paced the bay around a sharp turn and ran almost head-on into a tight group of coming riders before he heard them.

Trevannon yanked his horse around so swiftly the animal reared, nearly unseating him. He had only that glimpse of the dark shapes of horses and men in the beating rain, and then he spurred headlong into the flanking forest, hearing a heavily accented voice boom an order from bellows-like lungs. Vandermeer of course . . . the old law-dog knew the fugitives must cross the roads, doubtless had his posses distributed at every strategic point. He'd had the bad fortune to run into the sheriff's own group. . . .

Wes heard the crash of brush in his wake as the posse men followed into the timber. There was an outbreak of scattered shots, this ceasing at another bull-roared order by the sheriff. The men were milling disconcertedly through the trees; stray or ricocheting slugs could find anyone.

Trevannon tight-reined his first panicked reaction, forced himself to maneuver at a discreet pace through the wood. He didn't want to fight these men, nor would he be taken alive if he could avoid it; the bank job plus other blots on his backtrail would add to years in prison.

He cut suddenly from a straight flight into a right-angle turn and plunged across a glade into dripping underbrush. Dismounted in the dense foliage, held a hand over his horse's muzzle and waited. The sound of nearing pursuers grew; he caught sight of several through the trees; then they were past and the sounds of their going drifted away.

Trevannon rubbed a hand over his clammy face, his heart pounding painfully in his chest. Too close. Only cover of the storm's murk and noise had spared him certain capture. Now Vandermeer would concentrate his full effort on this area, infiltrate it and cordon it with men. Already a pale blaze along the horizon indicated a clearing sky as the storm clouds rocketed on toward the west. There were yet hours of daylight ahead.

One thing—he thinks you're pushing south now. But when he don't find your trail, he'll come back. Gives you a breathing space. Use it.

Trevannon turned due east and held to the timber till it became sparse and patchy. He could be easily spotted on these open flats, but for now he must think only of gaining distance. He lost track of time as the sky disgorged its final volley of wind and rain, as the steady rocking pace of his horse, held in to conserve its strength, became a monotonous cadence.

Leaving the last trees, he was puzzled to see a vast sweep of gray distance open before him and soon, a little farther on, he understood. This was a high tableland, and now he remembered hearing that its eastern edge ended above the rich grasslands of the lower county. From here the land dropped steeply away in rocky terraces to a distant valley floor. The first terrace slopes looked treacherous, but appeared to taper at a gentler grade toward the bottom. This would be tricky to negotiate, but he wanted to get off the flats; to turn back would almost certainly blunder him into another posse—of men who knew the terrain, who would harry him and drive his back to a wall.

He rode paralleling the rimrock, scanning its fallaway to the first terrace. It wasn't too steep at this point, but plainly laced with treacherous slides and potholes. A man afoot could traverse it easily, but a mounted man would be forced to dismount and lead his horse slowly and painstakingly to its base, repeating this pattern for the next several terraces.

Trevannon halted on the bank of a deep, broad wash, ordinarily dry, but now become a boiling torrent confined by its steep walls. Over ages of beating out a storm-fed track, the wash had scored deep into the rimrock and had worn a fairly easy slant down through the sharp upper terraces. In dry weather it might afford easy passage; to tackle it now would be to risk death by drowning, by being crushed with the flood's resistless force against the rocky banks.

He reined back from the wash, only to iron-hand his bay to a dead halt. Riders were leaving the fringe of timber he'd quitted, coming on without haste. Still perhaps a hundred yards distant, they'd have spotted him at once on the bare rim. Vandermeer had quickly divined his crude ruse, and had backtracked to simply follow out his broken trail through the brush.

They were in no hurry, fanning out in a broad line as they closed the gap. Trevannon made out the glint of drawn weapons, but they could afford to hold fire. Caught between the rim and a line of riders, he could only surrender, make a hopeless fight, or . . .

Wes made his decision. And savagely rammed steel into the bay's sides, launching it like an arrow toward the flooded gully. He heard a posse man's yell as he plunged down the bank. The bay's braced legs skidded stiffly against crumbling talus, then hit the current.

Feeling the animal's powerful surge of muscles as it fought for footing on the slick pebbly stream-bed, Trevannon was tensed for immediate disaster. And found to his surprise that the muddy flow swirled little more than fetlock-deep at this point.

He kicked the bay downstream. Directly ahead the banks pinched narrow and rose to form a wide, steep-walled gorge. The water deepened as it neared this increased confinement. Trevannon hesitated, was swiftly decided by the nearing drift of shouts as the posse swarmed toward the wash. He drove recklessly into the gorge, was quickly lost in its winding turns. The walls heightened; sharp twists cut off view ahead beyond a few yards. And now he knew a trapped and primitive panic as the walls continued to narrow and the flood gained depth and fury, threatening to sweep horse and rider like corks before it.

Suddenly the bay plunged to its knees in a hidden drop, then rolled ponderously sidelong. Trevannon kicked free of his stirrups, flung himself outward, and was immediately drenched. He staggered to his feet, choking and sputtering, grabbed the reins as the bay floundered to its feet. For a moment he faced down-gorge and his heart sank—the walls tapered to a crevice only a couple of yards wide into which the flood roared darkly.

The bay would be rushed off its feet if they went on . . . but the rain-fed waters were piling up swiftly behind. Ride it out to the bottom or be drowned . . . hope the gorge would peter out and widen on the lower levels. With this thought he toed into the stirrup, savagely squeezing the horse forward before he was securely in leather. The bay shied, but then lunged down the turgid channel. The walls closed about them with a solid, oppressive gloom, and the roar of water was a shattering echo.

As he felt the horse lose its fight for sound footing, Trevannon left the saddle and clung with a deathlike grip to his pommel. The horse churned frantically to avoid the flinty walls. An unseen abutment battered Trevannon's hurt shoulder, numbing it and his whole arm. He clung desperately to the horn with his good hand.

Suddenly the watery corridor widened; daylight showed a wide break ahead. At once the water lost force; Trevannon felt the bay's iron shoes grate as it clambered to solid rock underfoot. Again the walls tapered down to low banks. With a last rallied effort of his bruised and aching body, Trevannon heaved himself across the saddle and reined out of the shallowing flow, climbing a low hillock.

He reeled from his saddle and fell face down. Breathed into the wet earth and grass against his face and realized fully what he'd nearly forgotten so long ago . . . that life was a very good thing.

When he had regained his breath he rolled to a squatting position, took his bearings. He was on a midway terrace, past the worst of the steep upper heights. The lower terraces sloping gradually to the valley floor were covered by a heavy growth of trees and thickets that would cut him off from the plateau rim, and he could make his easy way to the bottom.

The pursuers would not follow, he felt certain; he doubted that even Vandermeer could rally any of the counterjumpers who composed his posse to continue the search. Their quarry had slipped through their grasp; they'd be wet, tired, disgusted, and busily convincing each other that he was a goner. Of course the sheriff himself would take no chance; when the gully ran dry, he'd search for the body.

Trevannon eased carefully to his feet. His upper body was a mass of bruises; pain tore savagely at his shoulder. He rubbed his right hip and then stiffened, frowning. He ripped open the slicker and found his pistol gone. Doubtless slipped from his holster when he'd flung himself from his falling horse up the gully.

He released an unsettled breath. At least he had killed any immediate pursuit. He could pick up another gun later—if he needed it. He hoped not; his decision from the dark road he'd forged out had been no whim. *Don't make yourself any promises outside that,* he cautioned himself now. *Life don't let a man deal his own hand. Pick up your cards as they fall.*

Wes mounted up again and took his way through the brush cover of the lower terraces, emerging onto the flats below which rolled gently away to gray-dim meadows and forests. He hit up a southeasterly route at a brisk clip, holding to belts of woodland till he was well beyond the plateau wall, and then struck out across rolling graze. A slight fever throbbed behind his temples and a burning thirst drove him to drain his canteen.

Shortly he hit a twisting, low-banked creek, but the water was roiled and muddy from the rains. He came down off the bay to kneel down and bathe his hot face, then noted that the last black clouds were drifting on; the storm was over. He paused long enough to shed his slicker and tie it behind his cantle. He emptied a saddlebag and transferred the sack of money to it, also his gunbelt and empty holster, cramming his belongings back on top and belting down the flap. Afterward he followed the stream, hoping it would bring him to a ranch headquarters or a settler's cabin. A hot meal and a night's sleep would put him back in shape, and he could secretly apply a decent dressing to his wound.

Time and again he spooked up bunches of shorthorn cattle grazing along the stream bottom. They were fat and moved sluggishly, and he noted the brand—KC. This, then, was the giant Kaysee ranch, actually a small cattle empire renowned throughout the territory, as was its owner, Kilrain Carter. His realm might be small as compared to John Chisum's, but his name was legendary in cattle country fame.

As he was wondering how near was the closest lineshack on this farflung range, Trevannon crested the brow of a rise and saw spread out below a vast labyrinth of corrals and buildings—Kaysee headquarters. He smiled wryly as he gigged the bay down the long slope, thinking that his brief visit here would add a minor tidbit to the campfire yarns spun about Kilrain Carter . . . of how a wounded bank-robber took advantage of the rancher's hospitality and rode on undetected.

Wes saw a wedge of mounted men, evidently the crew, splitting off from the working part of the layout on the side opposite to that where he was riding in. Evidently the crew was leaving their home base now the storm had passed.

Minutes later he cantered his horse across the deserted

compound between two big haysheds, intending to head for
the cookshack which he'd spotted from the slope. Then he
reined sharply in, at once nerve-strung and wary, as a
shotgun bellowed, its single blast beating down the afternoon stillness.

CHAPTER 3

AS THE BLACK CLOUDS DROVE ON TO THE EAST AND breaking sunlight swept away the iron pallor of their shadows before it, Andrea Carter stepped onto the roofed front veranda of Kaysee's big, jerry-built main house and breathed deeply of the sharp sweet air. She gave her husband a glance and an absent smile.

"A fine day after all, Kil."

Kilrain Carter glanced at his young wife with heavy-handed irony, grunted dryly, "Fine, now we get in a half day's work," and stomped off the veranda to head across to the corrals.

Andrea watched him go, feeling as she always did that sense of childish awe she might have felt for a stern grandparent. It wasn't only the more than thirty years' difference in their ages. Kilrain Carter was still a giant unbent by the time and trials that marked his harsh, rugged face. Imposing in leather *chaparejos,* a white broadcloth shirt with string tie, and a flat-crowned black Stetson with a sun-glittering hatband of silver conches, he looked what he was: a man who'd pulled himself by his bootstraps to solid power and prosperity. Andrea no longer thought much of the disparity in their ages, the lack of romance in their union, or even Kil's half-tolerant, half-disdainful treatment of her; she had come to lean on his solid, rooted-in-the-earth strength.

Her attention now strayed lightly to the small commotion

over by the breaking corral. The crew had already trooped
up from the bunkhouse; it looked as though Tige would
tackle that blue mustang today after all.

With a sense of eager thrill, Andrea hurried across the
drenched yard. She automatically avoided the puddles, the
skirt of her dark blue dress of watered silk lifted a few
discreet inches. It fitted her poised slimness perfectly, and
the shining auburn coils of her hair contrasted with the
faultless ivory of her complexion which sun and wind never
seemed to touch. Andrea knew exactly how she looked, was
attentive to every detail in her surface thoughts, and didn't
really care in the least.

She felt a certain naughty amusement at the way the
hands nudged each other as she approached—*keep the talk
clean, boys*. Kilrain Carter stood by with hands on hips,
looking on with thin patience; he wanted the crew on range,
but he always shrewdly gauged their moods. Push them to
the limit, but never tamper with their small pleasures; all
hands had looked forward to watching Tige Menefee break
the blue. Kil gave her an irritable glance, disliking her
presence here, but he said nothing—as though he read her
mood equally well. Andrea loved such spectacles.

She felt a man move to her side, identifying his rank,
sweat-sour smell before she glanced at him.

"Ought to be a great scrap, missus," Bill Treat observed,
his sly, milky stare flickering over her before settling on her
face.

Treat was a solid block of a man, not tall, in his early
forties. His cuffed-back Stetson showed a tight cluster of
flaxen-white hair above a broad and brutal face. That curly
forelock, Andrea always thought, completed the man's
likeness to a ringy bull. Yet his secretive ways confused her;
the blunt hungers he barely held in leash made her uneasy.

She started to reach for her heliotrope-scented handkerchief, checked the gesture, and smiled graciously. She
murmured, "I'm sure it will be, Mr. Treat," before moving
a step away from the stocky foreman. Mostly she considered him a minor unpleasantness which she avoided

when she could. Kilrain boasted of the man, called him the best damned ramrod in the territory, so she couldn't easily snub him. Treat showed his small icy grin and moved off.

Tige Menefee, the wrangler, stepped with fluid grace between the corral poles and walked to the snubbing post where a stable hand was holding the blue. Menefee was a white-Ute breed, a wiry, cat-flanked man whose mahogany-colored face was scored by a deep scar which pulled his mouth into a perpetual ugly grimace. Andrea felt his opaque eyes, like pools of shiny tar, swing briefly to rest on her, eyes that flickered for a moment with more than an Indian inscrutability. Andrea felt a quick warmth, as she might for an adoring pup. Tige's awed worship was much nicer than the attitude of that damned smelly foreman.

The big blue stood quietly, though every muscle in his body quivered with a wonderful activity beneath the shimmering, steel-blue coat. Tige cinched on a double-rigged Porter hull, adjusted a braided hackamore with its knot against the tender part of the horse's jaw. Tige could be cruel of necessity, but he had a sixth sense for horseflesh; as he worked, he spoke quietly to the animal in a silvery, flowing Indian dialect unlike his harsh, rarely-used English gutturals. Andrea could see how the animal steadied to his sensitive hands and voice; getting saddle and bridle on an unbroken horse could be a savage chore in itself. Tige had hardly bothered to condition the blue to the gear perviously, yet he had it on in seconds.

Tige was in the saddle with a graceful twist; he nodded to the stable hand, who whipped off the blindfold, let the horse go, and raced for the safety of the fence. . . .

It was a magnificent thing to watch, the blue starting off with a bucking so savage that for the first minute he hardly touched the ground. Then he sunfished and reared high, almost going over backward; but Tige, as though reading his bluff, held the saddle. Then he lunged against the fence, would have crushed Tige's leg to a pulp if the half-breed hadn't unstirruped his right foot in easy anticipation and swung it high out of danger.

Andrea watched wide-eyed, lips parted. Bitter dust stung her nostrils. She felt the craze-paced excitement of the duel race like a fiery torrent through her blood. She could know for these moments exactly the unleashed emotions that her mother had always warned her to keep in check. For an instant, one shocked thought poured through her naked mind, sloughed of her usual restless, shifting surface moods—*is this what a woman is supposed to feel for a man?*

Even the iron-constitutioned Tige began to show the strain of battle, but so did the blue. It was wheezing savagely, coat lathered with dirty froth, as it fought its final token plays against a burrlike rider who outmaneuvered it at every turn. When it came to a shivering standstill, Tige slipped to the ground, ignoring the crew's wild cheers as he tended to the jaded animal, at once throwing off the saddle and bridle, always talking to it in silvery Ute.

Andrea walked slowly up to the house, put her back against a fluted porch column. The tense tumult still held within her. She watched Kilrain give brisk orders to Bill Treat, and the crew dispersed to saddle their horses. Kilrain swung about and tramped up to the house, paused by the veranda to remove his hat and swipe a broad fist across his graying cowlick. For a moment they stood in silence, watching the crew ride out. A silence broken by the low, imploring call of Andrea's mother from the front parlor:

"Andrea, dear—"

"The old lady's calling you," Kilrain said without looking at her.

Andrea shrugged carelessly. "Let her call. It'll be 'Andrea, bring my shawl,' or some other silly triviality. . . ."

He did look at her then, slowly and appraisingly. "I can remember when you jumped every time your old lady breathed hard. Not so long ago, either."

Andrea's dark violet eyes met his softly. "People do change, my dear."

He snorted, clamping his hat back on. "Not your mother. By God, she's a real princess."

"After all," Andrea remonstrated sweetly, "when you married me—"

"I didn't marry your rattler-tongued mama," he observed harshly. "Damned if she wouldn't make a regiment of mother-in-laws."

"Oh, Kil, really . . ."

"All right, all right," Kilrain Carter said wearily. "She's a cripple, a proud one too—no fault of hers. And you're a pretty little showpiece of a wife; I never bargained for more; at my age, a man's earned a right to make a fool of himself. Still, I ain't a patient man, particular for her high-falutin' ways."

He added dryly, "Pass the word."

Andrea nodded mechanically, caught up always by the blunt force of her husband's personality. She didn't suppose she'd ever love him as a woman should, but it was so easy to cling to his strength. . . .

She leaned toward him glowingly. "Kilrain—"

He made a brusque gesture that cut her off; she followed his glance across the yard. A strange figure of a man had come into view from around a hayshed, shambling afoot toward the house. Kilrain grunted his contempt. "That fool half-wit, Bodie Teece."

"What does he want?" Andrea wondered.

Kilrain laughed sourly. "To tell me again how I'm damned to eternal perdition. Make more threats he ain't got the sand to follow through. Hell, you heard him before."

"Yes"—Andrea shivered, though the humid air was already warm—"but he always . . . frightens me. What a strange little man!"

She knew the story—of how, six months ago, some of the Kaysee cowboys on a Saturday night whoop-up had hoorawed a revivalist meeting presided over by Bodiah Teece, a fiery evangelist belonging to the strange sect who called themselves the Canaanites. In frenzied rage, Teece had tried to drag a rider from his horse. A flailing hoof had accidentally caught the little man in the head. He'd lain between life and death for a month, and when he'd regained a semblance of his senses, had blamed Kilrain Carter, the cowboys' boss, for the disorder. It must have been his last clear thought before he was struck in the head, and afterward it had obsessed him always. He visited the ranch periodically to rail at the rancher, swearing that the Lord would exact vengeance for the blasphemy against his servant, which always vastly amused Kilrain Carter.

Now Teece halted a few paces away, a wiry runt in a greasy elkhide coat and pants which flapped in tatters around his skinny shanks. The sun polished his saintly ruff of cloudy white hair to a golden nimbus around his hawk-lean head. Over one arm he carried a heavy shotgun; this wasn't part of his customary appearance when he was "out to raid Hell," as Kilrain put it.

"Hello, Bodie," Kilrain drawled now, humorously. "Get Satan in your sights lately?"

Teece pointed a bony, trembling finger at him. "Devil's spawn! Citizen of Gomorrah! I have finally learned how you mock the Lord and make league with His Enemy . . . and now may He have mercy on your black soul."

He spoke with a cold, quiet fervor unlike his usual raving; some note in it made Andrea shiver. Kilrain also recognized it; his voice hardened. "Get out, you old lunatic. Come back again, I'll have you horsewhipped off the place."

Teece didn't move. His vague and watery eyes blazed with the hot zeal that gripped him. The shotgun rose to center on Kilrain's broad chest. The rancher's fist knotted, and he took a step forward.

Teece did not hesitate. The buckshot charge took Kilrain Carter full in the chest and smashed him backward. A porch column caught him in the back, and he slid down in a sitting position. He looked bewilderedly at Andrea and his lips moved, then he pitched sideward and was motionless.

Andrea's trancelike stare moved to Bodie Teece. The little madman's attention was already fixing her with its crazed intensity. "Woman, the wrath of the living God is a dreadful thing . . . there is no getting out of His mighty hand!" The twin muzzles of the shotgun veered a little to bear on her. "I know you, wanton. All the evil of the world is bound into your nature—Delilah, Salome, *Jezebel*!"

Andrea heard the frightened voice of her mother. "Andrea! Andrea, what is it?" She tried to speak, but her throat worked soundlessly.

Teece took a long step and the shotgun muzzles touched her breast. She recoiled a little, looking down at the sooty smudge left on her bodice. It seemed to release her voice. Her scream hung like a bright keen blade in the warm air.

As the shotgun shattered the ranchyard quiet, Trevannon reined in to place the sound, at once wishing he had his gun. A man might be shooting at quail or rabbit, but his was the taut wariness of a hunted man, even knowing as he did that no word could have yet gone ahead. . . .

Then a woman's scream, holding a note of pure terror. At once he spurred hard past the barns, veered around a carriage shed, and pulled his mount up in a long yard fronting a big, rambling house. For an instant the scene froze him . . . a man sprawled face down by the veranda, another man with a shotgun pointed at a young woman.

The ragged little fellow came instantly about, the shotgun arcing with his turn, training on Trevannon. "Tryin' to sneak up on old Teece, eh, bucko!" he cackled.

Trevannon did not twitch a muscle, not missing the hair-trigger wildness in the man's ravaged face or the shotgun with one hammer back-eared and ready.

"Easy, Pop," he counseled softly. "Stranger. Looking for food and a bed."

The faded, wicked gaze swept him. "Ahh . . . stranger. But this is no Christian place, man; in it you'll find scant rest and sour eating. Turn your animal and leave, before its godless taint touches you."

Baffled by Teece's evangelizing pulpit manner, Trevannon nodded at the man on the ground, saying, "He hurt, or—?"

Instantly the little man's half-mollified gaze flamed; his bony fists white-knuckled around the shotgun. "He has felt the mailed fist of God; vengeance is mine, saith the Lord!"

From within the house came a woman's voice, quavering plaintively, "Andrea . . . Andrea, what is it, what's wrong?" The girl said nothing, staring blankly at Trevannon, her face sheet-white.

Trevannon felt the alien chill a man knows on finding himself face to face with madness. With a maniac whose crazed impulses were plainly dancing on the edge of new violence. And at this range that heavy-guage weapon would cut him from the saddle like a rag doll. Through a dry throat, he forced drawling calm into his words. "Sounds like he was the devil's hairpin, sure enough. Obliged to you for the good word, Reverend."

At once the edged danger in Teece's expression faded, replaced by a childish pleasure. He even lowered the shotgun. "Your eyes are clear . . . God-fearing eyes. They know His spokesman!" The crafty care of a madman marked his next words. "Good, but now leave—wait. You have a gun?"

"Saddle gun."

"Drop it to the ground."

Under that watchful and glinting eye, Trevannon slowly slipped his carbine from its scabbard, let it fall.

Teece motioned jerkily with his weapon. "Now leave. The Lord's justice is not complete."

Wes started to quarter his animal around, lifting the reins, and Teece at once swung back toward the girl, the shotgun leveled.

"Now your reckoning, woman!"

Trevannon cantered the bay a few paces away, reaching down to unfix his lariat from the pommel. Silently he shook out the coils. With dexterous ease he whirled out a loop, at the same time boot-nudging the bay around.

Warned by the sudden break in the horse's pace, Teece

glanced over his shoulder. Shrilled a gibbered curse and began to swing around. Trevannon had already made his cast; as the noose cleared Teece's hatbrim he slammed in the spurs, lunging the bay away.

Teece was bringing the shotgun to bear as the rope snapped taut; there was a sickening sound as his light frame was yanked from its feet. The shotgun's second barrel went off, pointing down; a geyser of mud erupted from the yard. Teece's body mucked out a furrow five yards long before Trevannon could drag the bay to a halt.

Wes swung down and ran to the crumpled form. He started to bend over, then straightened, swallowing against a hot sourness boiling into his throat. Teece's neck was bent at a grotesque, impossible angle.

Dimly he heard the woman in the house moaning weakly, "Andrea . . . Andrea, please." The girl stood rooted, her eyes fixed on Trevannon and beyond him. Suddenly she began to laugh, quietly and almost bemusedly.

Trevannon tramped across to her, intending to shake her out of it. Before he reached her, the laughter ceased as abruptly as it had begun. Her violet eyes focused on his with a cool innocence that reminded him of a child's shocking inability to comprehend tragedy. Her voice was as light and calm as a summer day.

"Thank you, sir. You saved my life."

CHAPTER 4

"RECKON KAYSEE'LL BE HERS NOW."

"And that'll be the end. The Old Man was hard-headed as a ten-penny spike, but her and the old lady . . . The crazy Congreves. It'll run through their fingers like sand."

"I dunno . . . reckon I'd take odds on the old lady Give her a free hand, she'll be hell on wheels."

"Hell, yes! She damn near shoved the girl into Kil's bed to marry into the ranch. Only Kil wasn't as much of an old fool as she guessed. Kept the both of 'em in their place. Well, the Old Man's gone to his Maker, that gives Old Lady Congreve the free hand you mentioned. The girl'll be owner in name only."

"Still, took a lot of *hombre* to hold together a spread like the Kaysee. Old Kil was the man. Lord. Who'd ever thought he'd go like that, crazy sky pilot busting him in two with a load of double-ought buck?"

"Like I said . . . I'll take odds on the old lady."

"Be trouble for sure, shooting trouble, when the word gets out. Our open range'll go up for grabs. For a plugged nickel, I'd take my time, quit."

"What the hell, job's a job. I'll stick. . . ."

Trevannon stood outside the bunkhouse, leaning against the trunk of a big cottonwood whose spreading boughs shadowed him. Staring at the lamplit rectangle of the open bunkhouse doorway and listening to the crew's low voices. Frowning, he drew on his cigarette, felt it scorch his fingers

29

and pinched it out. He swung restlessly away from the tree
and lounged across the yard, widely skirting the house
beneath its parklike canopy of cottonwoods.

Casting back on this long, violence-crowded day, Trevannon found little to cheer about. A damned poor new
beginning for a man, with a robbery and two killings on his
conscience. Yet he'd killed once in self-defense, then to
save a girl from being murdered in cold blood. . . . No
man could choose the hand that was dealt him, and in these
circumstances regret was a futile kind of self-pity.

He was more than a little puzzled by Andrea Carter. Her
beauty was that of a diamond, cold and hard and unattainable. Even in cowtown bordellos you met such women,
frozen behind their own glacial beauty, using their bodies
and faces like tools. Yet, he thought, this wasn't Andrea's
trouble, or at best only part of it. He remembered how when
he'd roped and dragged Teece, she had begun a whimpered
hysteria as though she'd wholly lost her grip, only to
assume an instant later a polite composure that would have
been ice-blooded, except for the complete and genuine
innocence of it. As if several people inhabited her body at
once, any one of these coming to the fore at an instant's
notice. . . . Damned strange.

Though no reason to concern himself, Trevannon
thought; at first dawn he'd be on his way south. He had
rolled into an empty bunk in the bunkhouse for a spell, but
his charged thoughts had kept him awake. Maybe he could
sleep after he had worried it all out.

The shotgun blasts had brought back the crew on the
gallop, and Wes had noted how the ramrod, Bill Treat, had
at once commandeered the situation. Behind the man's
sober regret had lurked a sly, expanding pleasure that hadn't
escaped Trevannon. A man who'd risen to ramrod an outfit
like this one certainly lacked neither competence nor
ambition, but while Kilrain Carter had lived, there would
have been only one voice of authority on Kaysee. Obviously Treat saw himself liberated by the rancher's death,

perhaps, judging by the drift of his attentions, as a comforter of the grieving widow.

Trevannon smiled faintly; he had met Andrea Carter's mother. Treat was likely due for a rude check on his rocketing designs. Kaysee would doubtless need Bill Treat, now more than ever, but as to any bargain achieved when that old lady and the blustering, officious foreman locked wills . . . like the odds-taking puncher, he'd bet on Mrs. Congreve. Treat had gone up to the big house directly from the cookshack after supper, and they were likely debating the situation now . . . with the body of Kaysee's late owner beneath the same roof, not yet stiff in death.

A strange lot, these Kaysee people, Wes decided with only faint repugnance; he had met all kinds. He stirred his shoulders in a faint shrug, winced as his wound throbbed to fresh life. He had got off by himself long enough to clean it with a whiskey-soaked swab and apply a better bandage. It would do for a hurt so slight; he'd received less care for old war lead he still carried.

His slow pacing had brought him to the west fringe of the grove and he paused there, facing the open yard that sided the big house. Heard voices that brought his gaze to the fancy French windows from which warm lampglow spilled onto a broad stone patio. He saw Andrea Carter step outside with her easy, statuesque grace—Bill Treat's powerful, bull-built form moving close to her elbow. Their words carried clearly through the windless, still darkness.

"Whyn't you call me Bill, Miz Carter? You been here nigh a year, this thing sort of pulls us Kaysee people together, if you see what I mean."

Andrea paused and fanned herself with a handkerchief, the tilt of her head abstracted as she looked out into the night, hardly paying attention to Treat's crude solicitude.

"Miz Carter?" Treat said softly, an irritated note to it.

"Oh—oh, pardon me. Yes, that will be fine."

Treat moved around the girl and half-faced her to get her attention. "Now, ma'am, I ain't likin' to right off intrude on your sorrow with business, but it's sorta necessary. Outfit like Kaysee can't afford takin' even a day off for mournin'. Hard fact, but that's so."

"Yes, I suppose so," Andrea said distantly.

"Good. Sensible of you." Treat spoke more briskly. "Let's get to cases. The old gray wolf is dead, and the coyotes'll be circlin' in shortly to divide the spoils."

Andrea did look at him now, aroused from her indifference. "I don't understand. . . ."

"I mean them sodbusters over on the East Bench," Treat said harshly. "This spring they tried to homestead some choice range of ourn. We batted their ears down. Burned their shacks, drove 'em off. They were dead leary of our outfit afterward. . . . But ma'am, Kilrain Carter *was* Kaysee, and the whole territory knew it. With him gone, I make it them sodders'll try to push back, try hard."

"I see," she said slowly. "Well . . . what do you think?"

"I think we should hit them before they hit us. Show 'em nothin's changed. I'll hand-pick a bunch of the crew tomorrow, boys who know this kind of fight. Take 'em over to the Bench, push the sodders around a little, enough to give 'em the idea."

"Oh," she faltered. "Do you think you should?"

"Ma'am," Treat said in a soft, positive way, "it occur to you that Mr. Carter's death might not have been no accident—that it was planned?"

"Oh no," Andrea protested emphatically. "You didn't see that old man before Mr. Trevannon stopped him. He was *crazy,* clear out of his mind. Nobody could have planned that—"

"Think a minute. Them sodders are Canaanites, that religious bunch old Bodie was always preachin' for. Their leader is Ephraim Waybeck, and his wife is Bodie Teece's sister. Sure, Bodie's grudge agin Mr. Carter was never more'n crazy talk—but if someone close to Bodie worked on him long enough, talked some guts into him—he'd've been pushed to this killin'. Be perfect. Old Bodie and his crazy grudge would get blamed, and whoever egged him on

would be in the clear. Like I say—Kilrain Carter was
Kaysee. You tell me who had better reason for wantin' him
dead so's they could grab that chunk of Kaysee range."

"Oh . . . there *was* something that Teece said before
he—but I didn't think. . . . Do you really believe that the
Canaanites would—"

"Sure, sure," Treat snapped impatiently. "I know.
They're always talkin' peace an' brotherhood, stuff like
that. That's nothin' but talk, believe me. You seen what that
religion done to old Teece. Why, lady, they're a pack of
blood-mad dogs; you muzzle your mad dogs before they
bite you. Or shoot them." He paused. "Then there's old
Cass McQuayle, the lawyer. He's the one who talked
Ephraim Waybeck's people into filing homesteads on a
chunk of the Kaysee. I always made it he had some private
reason for wantin' 'em on that land. Maybe enough reason
to want Mr. Carter dead as much as them."

"I don't think that's right. Mr. McQuayle seems like a
very nice old man."

"All right," Treat said exasperatedly. "But someone
talked up a storm to Bodie Teece to make him gun your
husband. McQuayle and the Canaanites had the motive—I
say hit 'em before they hit us!"

Andrea pressed a hand to her temple. "I—I don't know,"
she said helplessly. "This has all happened so
quickly. . . ."

Listening, Trevannon grudgingly gave Treat a point: the
foreman was shrewd enough to work on the girl rather than
on her mother. He'd succeeded in arousing her from her
apathy of indecision; now he quickly pressed the advantage,
speaking with an air of great sincerity.

"I know, Miz Carter. I know, believe me. Rough, sure,
but it's for the best." He paused, his glinting stare intent on
her face; his tongue flicked his lips. "They got to know
who's boss, you see. Got to know a man has stepped into
Kilrain Carter's boots. That man can be me. Just say the
word."

Trevannon recognized the double meaning behind the

foreman's words, the lust half-spoken. Treat was too crude, too full of huge, uncomplicated appetites that were driving him further than he'd intended. Andrea only stared at him wordlessly. Her sophisticated way of dress and speech were but surface details of her nature, and she wasn't so much shocked as naïvely surprised.

Not reading her silence correctly, Treat reached and caught her by the upper arms, his face slack with primal hunger he could no longer conceal. He said hoarsely, "It can be, ma'am. Just say the word—"

"No!" Andrea twisted out of his grasp. "Go away—get back to the bunkhouse. Don't ever touch me again."

As it did in men like Treat, desire blazed into a feral rage. "Why you—damned little teaser—"

Andrea thrust out her arms as though to hold him off, backing fearfully away. A stone bench caught her behind the knees and she sat down, Treat hulking above her. Trevannon had already left the grove and was loping across the yard in long strides. As his boots grated on the patio flagstones, Treat came about to face him. The foreman's great shoulders were hunched, his pale eyes burnished with bright, wild fury.

"No mix of yours, saddle bum!"

"You're a pig," Trevannon said quietly. "Back to your sty."

With a throat-deep snarl, Treat moved in toward him. Trevannon had several inches of reach on the thickset foreman and he used it, stepping easily back from Treat's first wild swing, then driving a straight hard right into the man's mouth. Treat backpedaled; blood broke darkly from his split lip. He touched it and his blind rage drained away, replaced by a cold, calculated urge to kill. Trevannon saw it in his face, stepped back as Treat stooped and tugged at his boot.

His hand came up with eight inches of gleaming steel yanked from a concealed boot-sheath—one of the slim, straight-edged knives called an Arkansas Toothpick. Dexterously Treat flipped it in his palm so that the blade pointed outward. Trevannon sank to a crouch and pivoted slowly to keep facing the foreman as Treat began a slow circling of him. Andrea Carter shrank against the stone bench, a hand at her throat.

Treat lunged. Instead of leaping back, Trevannon stepped lightly aside, let the knife pass between his body and left arm, then clamped that arm tight to his side, pinning Treat's at the elbow. Treat slammed into him with a grunt, bounded back from Trevannon's spraddle-legged stance; Wes brought his right fist up between them, a pile-driver that rocked Treat's head back on his short neck. Treat's knees melted, but Trevannon held him upright, caught Treat's knife-arm at the wrist and slammed it across his own lifted knee. The foreman howled with pain; the knife clattered to the flagstones. Trevannon set a palm against his chest and shoved. Treat pitched backward into the bushes that hedged the patio, thrashed frantically there as he cursed in his rage and pain.

Trevannon bent and picked up the knife, drove it into the interstice between two flagstones and pushed it sideways. The blade snapped off an inch below the cross-guard. Wes tossed the handle away and straightened as Treat disentangled himself from the shrubbery.

He faced the tall, gaunt drifter, panting and rubbing his mouth. His eyes blazed undiluted hatred.

"Another time, bum," he whispered. "You got me by surprise. Another time."

"Keep telling yourself that."

The foreman spun on a heel and stalked from the patio, heading for the bunkhouse. Timidly the girl touched Trevannon's arm, but drew back as he looked at her.

"I owe you for twice now," she said softly. For a moment her eyes glowed with a womanly fullness. Then they sparked with a little-girl petulance. "That Bill Treat. He's so smelly and dirty. I hate men who are like that."

CHAPTER 5

As Andrea stepped back through the French doors into the big parlor, her mother's wheel chair propelled silently into the room from the hallway that branched off between the bedrooms.

"Help me to the divan, please, Andrea," Mrs. Congreve said crisply. Her hands, clawed over the iron wheels of the chair, now reached tremblingly for the hickory cane that lay across her lap. With its aid, and Andrea's, she slowly stood and limped to the leather divan, settling onto its worn cushions.

She remained bolt upright, her hands still gripping the cane, her black, fiercely snapping eyes surveying her daughter with a grave and merciless attention. Mrs. Congreve was still in her mid-forties, but so far as Andrea could remember she had always been a miniature and withered woman with dead white hair in a tight bun, had always affected the black prim gowns she wore. She was delicately boned with skin like transparent parchment. Her thin, autocratic face was ravaged by pain that was no sham; Andrea had seen the misshapen horror of her twisted legs only once, as a child—a memory that had haunted her dreams for years.

"There was trouble?" she asked in the brittle, toneless manner that always put a listener on the defensive.

"That nasty foreman," Andrea said with a shudder. "I don't know why you left me alone with him."

"Very simple. He had something on his mind, and he was too shrewd to let it be known while I was present. So I left you alone."

"Oh . . . well, why don't we get up a party now? We can dance around Kilrain's coffin. Poor Mother, you can't dance."

"Irony does not become you, my dear," Mrs. Congreve said calmly. "Bill Treat is a belligerent, unwashed animal— but not a fool. He was right about one thing. That old lunatic could have been goaded into murdering your husband."

"You were listening in the hallway," Andrea accused sulkily.

Her mother ignored the interruption and went on musingly, "And you, my poor blind child, never saw what Treat and I see clearly . . . that Lawyer McQuayle's benevolent airs and mock mantle of righteousness are nothing but a pose. A benefactor of mankind, eh? Bah. I met him when we lived in Coldbrook. The man's a scheming opportunist. I think he got to Bodie Teece— Please pay attention, dear—"

"Mother!" Andrea screamed softly. *"Will* you stop treating me like a child?"

"You are a child, my sweet—a little girl in a woman's body. What do you expect—Andrea!"

Andrea had angrily turned her back and walked to the oak liquor cabinet; she took out a decanter of Kilrain's French brandy. She filled a tumbler, spilling some liquor in her haste, and drank it facing her mother, meeting her eyes defiantly across the glass rim.

Mrs. Congreve waited till Andrea had lowered the tumbler, gasping from the raw burning that scoured her throat and stomach, then said imperturbably, "Exactly what I mean. The act of a bellicose brat. It proves nothing. Come here and sit down."

Andrea did not move, but her gaze faltered away. "You have gotten out of hand since your marriage to Kilrain Carter," Mrs. Congreve went on softly. Andrea shut her eyes tightly, wishing she could silence that calm and hateful voice. "Because you had him to lean on, you proceeded to ignore my natural authority—as your mother." *Shut up, Mother, will you shut up!* ". . . . Kilrain is dead, you little fool. And you can no more stand alone than you can fly. A woman, a real woman, would have Bill Treat crawling at her feet. God knows what would have happened a minute ago if that drifter hadn't interceded. If you can't handle an elemental brute like Treat, what chance would you stand with a man wise in the ways of women? You're now legal mistress of Kaysee. For how long? Very briefly— unless I tell you what to do." She rapped her cane on the floor. *"Come here to me, Andrea."*

As though in a trance, Andrea moved to the divan and sank slowly onto it, staring at her hands in her lap. Her mother was silent now, evidently ferreting out the situation in her mind, and Andrea scarcely noticed. . . .

It had been this way between them as far as Andrea's memory reached. Her childhood was a dim and shadowy thing, with scant remembrance of a father. Of him, she had only her mother's iron judgment: that marrying Curt Congreve was the single great mistake of her life. Martha Godwin had come of a fine Boston family; at eighteen she had run off to the West with a poor dockhand whose ne'er- do-well ways had seemed romantic to a young girl—then. Only when the couple had settled down to raise cattle on the south end of this valley had the shiftless stupidity of Curt's bedrock nature become apparent. He was a "born fail- ure"—the cardinal sin in Martha's book. The ranch ran down, the cattle ran wild, Curt never got around to building a permanent house in place of the soddy where their infant daughter was born.

And Curt started drinking; Andrea could guess why, knowing her mother's cool, deadly way of making you feel abysmally guilty. Curt was drunk the night he drove his wife to the nearby settlement of Coldbrook when she felt her time coming again. He missed a turn in the badly rutted road, careened the buckboard into a deep gully, and crawled unhurt from its wreckage while Martha Congreve lay screaming with her lower body pinned beneath a kicking tangle of horses and harness. The bones were splintered beyond proper mending, though the nerves were miraculously intact—enough to insure Martha a lifetime of agony, as the doctor said later in town. Just before he operated to deliver her dead child . . . But not before Curt Congreve walked out into the alley and shot himself in the head. Thus sparing, as Martha Congreve often put it, a great deal of unpleasantness all around. . . .

Dr. MacKinnon—Doctor Mack—was a gruff bachelor who hated matrimony but loved children. He gladly took in four-year-old Andrea, and her mother became an efficient light housekeeper for the doctor after she learned to maneuver a wheel chair. Doctor Mack was rarely home, spending much of his time at his office or on house calls, leaving Martha Congreve a free hand with her daughter. Dimly Andrea saw how her mother had carefully kept her a child, teaching her to rely always on Mother, warning her against the pitfalls into which foolishly independent people fall. *Always stay close to Mother; be safe.* And later: *Andrea, never trust a man. If he offers you gifts, take them; it's no more than he owes for the heartbreak his kind causes all women. When he speaks of love, he means he wants your body. Therefore give him only your body, not your heart—or he will break it.*

Carefully shielded from every experience of awakening womanhood, Andrea was well set in the pattern by the time she was eighteen. During this time she was also carefully instructed by her mother in walking, grammar, dress and all the expected accomplishments of a Boston debutante. These were thoroughly ingrained, with her mother's other teachings, when the old doctor suddenly died. For a time they lived off the small legacy of his savings. In the evenings, they enjoyed mother-and-daughter chats:

"I saw you talking on the sidewalk today with Kilrain Carter, Andrea. What did he say?"

"Oh, Mother, he's such an old man."

"A wealthy old man . . . and not too old. I want you to

watch for him when he comes to town . . . make it your business to encounter him."

"But Mother. . . ."

"I'll tell you what to say. A woman's conversation, gracious and poised."

"But Mother, all he wants to talk about is cattle and horses."

"Little idiot, that's a rough, bluff bachelor's way of approaching you. He's fended off marriage these many years; he feels immune. But no man is immune. He'll expect an easy conquest of a starry-eyed girl. They all do. But you'll settle for nothing less than marriage; *I'll* see to that. First, get him to talk about himself. . . ."

It was six months in the doing—a hundred teasing offensives which Andrea performed by rote, a mechanically perfected wedding trap into which Kilrain Carter walked stolidly—and not so blindly. As he later told Andrea in his roughly mocking way, "Honey, nobody had me fooled. If I couldn't get you no other way, this suited me. Besides . . . got to thinking I'll need a son to carry on. Man thinks about those things at my age. And I'm a great believer in breedin'—horses, cattle, or people. That Boston blood of yours'll add a little sugar to the starch. I'm even endowin' thee with all my worldly goods to hold for the kid, case I pass on before he gets of age. . . ."

But there had been no son . . . there would be no son. And now, glancing sidelong at her mother and seeing the musing calculation unmasked in her face, Andrea realized in a rare moment of insight how Martha Congreve must have hoped for something like this. While Kil's driving personality had dominated Kaysee, she could never be more than a crippled and helpless object of Kilrain Carter's charity. And she had lost her hold on Andrea. The pressure of a maniac's finger on a shotgun trigger had given her back her daughter and all the old dreams of wealth and position, the birthright she had foolishly discarded.

A shocking thought came on the heels of that insight: *You don't have to do anything she says. Why, you own Kaysee now, you can send her away.* The thought brought a crushing fright from which Andrea shrank. . . .

"Andrea!"

Her mother's voice was brittle-sharp and Andrea looked at her quickly. Saw the satisfaction in her mother's seldom shown half-smile, and knew she'd reached some decision. "This man, Andrea—the saddle tramp, Wes Trevannon—I took a careful look at him this afternoon. I liked what I saw."

Andrea's thoughts veered warmly to the tall drifter. "Oh, I liked him too!" she said impulsively. "He looked so terrible when he was helping me—twice, you know—but then he was so quiet and kind you wouldn't think he was the same—"

"Andrea!" Mrs. Congreve snapped. "I am not interested in his gentle qualities—nor do I want you to be. Do you understand me?"

Andrea nodded wearily.

"What interested me," Mrs. Congreve went on thoughtfully, "was a sense of confidence, of quiet strength you could actually feel in the man. A sense of tragedy, too. But that in no way impairs a conviction he lends of being able to handle any physical or strategical situation. Which he certainly did, first saving your life with quick thinking, and then handling Bill Treat like a child in his arms. And he's a cowman; his whole appearance says as much. . . . Yes, I think that no man could easily outmaneuver Mr. Trevannon. A woman," she added softly, "might."

"What?"

"It's very simple. Shortly Kaysee's enemies will be circling in for the kill, as Bill Treat said. Not only the farmers, but small ranchers who were roughly treated by Kilrain over the years. Now Treat might be good enough to stop them, or he might not. He had, I think, a handy notion when he advised roughing up the squatters on the East Bench. If cowardly pacifists like the Canaanites could move in on us and get away with it—and I've little doubt they'll try—how can we stop the others?" Mrs. Congreve paused significantly. "There is obviously a better man than Treat to block this thing before it starts."

"Oh no," Andrea began to protest.

"Oh yes. Wes Trevannon will be Kaysee's new foreman." Mrs. Congreve stated it flatly, leaving not a jot of doubt.

"But—he might not want the job."

"Money is always a good argument. Reinforced by your charms, it should be a most telling one. The grieving, lovely widow who needs help . . . a few pleading tears shed . . . and you can tell he's a man who was raised to respect women. A rare sort, I might add. You could win Bill Treat over by earthier means—but you are a respectable widow now, my dear, and my plans for you do not include letting that swine paw you."

Of course not, Andrea thought dully, *damaged goods can't be used again.* Vaguely she wondered how she could be aware that she was her mother's pawn and yet lack the strength to break away. . . .

"Look outside," Martha Congreve commanded. "Is he still out there?"

Andrea walked to the French windows and looked out toward the grove. She saw the red firefly of a cigarette coal, and, by straining her eyes, made out Trevannon's tall form.

"He's just standing—smoking. Over by the trees."

"Good. Listen carefully, and I'll tell you exactly what to say. How to act."

CHAPTER 6

BREAKFAST IN THE COOKSHACK WAS A LONG-DRAWN AFFAIR because Bill Treat ate very slowly, forcing each mouthful between swollen, sausage-thick lips. He cursed once when he tried his coffee, left the scalding brew untouched. Afterward he held a black silence. The crew dawdled over their food and matched the foreman's taciturnity, carefully not looking at him. Though not troubling to conceal shuttling glances of curiosity at the unmarked face of the man who'd whipped him.

Wes Trevannon sat at the foot of the table with his long legs crossed, slumped in his chair, an arm slung over its back. His other hand held a cigarette which he'd absently rolled and lighted while brooding into his wiped-up plate. He mulled over his situation, ignored Treat and the crew.

Last evening Andrea Carter's offer of the job had caught him off-balance. She had approached him with a cool and decisive poise which contrasted to her previous childishly shifting moods. He couldn't tell whether that poise was real or simulated. If her mother had primed the girl, she'd done a remarkably convincing job. Andrea had mingled the offer of a breathtaking wage with a soft appeal to her defenseless womanhood that had touched him in spite of its probable calculation. Also his reaction was tempered by his new-found facing of himself . . . there was nothing sorrier than human putty warped by a bad mold. That girl needed help far beyond having a ranch saved. He couldn't frame this impression too well, even to himself, but one fact stood out strongly: these were two near-helpless women in a man's world, and he was a Texan and a Southerner. Every instinct of his upbringing swayed him.

Yet, almost curtly, he'd told her he would sleep on it, and then had headed for the bunkhouse. He had slept poorly enough, but by morning he'd made his decision.

He had to stop running sometime, had to make a start somewhere; why not here, where there was a need? A fugitive's first instinct had prompted him to put miles between himself and the mule-tenacious sheriff of Cedar Wells County. But during the night he had considered it out carefully. His face had been masked during the holdup; he was certain that no posse man had had a clear sight of him in the storm meeting. Even his horse, a solid-color bay with no distinctive markings, could not be certainly identified, and he could ride a different animal for a time. Word of how Kaysee had acquired a new foreman could not fail to reach Vandermeer and trigger his suspicion—but a lawman like Vandermeer would arrest no man without scrupulous evidence.

And evidence hinged solely on that grain sack of bank money. This Trevannon had buried beneath the clay floor in a corner of the harness shed when he had left his saddle there yesterday. That was a safe hiding place till he found a way to anonymously return the money to its bank. A man won no self-respect by halfway measures; if there were any guts to his reforming, he must make it clear-cut and decisive. The money was not his, and it would be returned.

With that decision he had to wryly remind himself against his first smug satisfaction: *You're no saint, never were, never will be. But you can look at yourself in a shaving mirror again of a morning. And that, by God, is something. . . .*

"Stayin' on a spell, mister?"

The casual question from the man at his elbow broke the

near silence. Trevannon glanced up, as did every man in the room. The questioner was a wolf-lean and grizzled man with a be-damned-to-you spunk in his faded eyes that Trevannon had noted and liked. If part of these oak-tough men's discreet silence was due to the shadowy wariness of their squat, brutal foreman, this old man didn't share it.

Bill Treat had paused in the act of lifting a forkful of griddlecake to his mouth. Trevannon met his hating stare a moment and thought coldly then, *No point putting it off.* There would be trouble for certain, but he guessed that it would come from Treat alone. Since it couldn't be side-stepped, it would do the crew good to watch it. A soft and evasive authority would never impress such men.

"Expect to be around quite a time." Trevannon ground out the cigarette in his plate as he spoke, met Treat's look squarely.

Treat set his thick, hairy hands on the table and half rose. He grinned frostily. "Wrong. You'll drift, bum. Now. Or be carried off after a sound horsewhippin'—"

"Why, Bill," the old man broke in with whimsical dryness, "that's plumb poor return for what this fella did. Put Carter's killer dead to rights—"

"Shut up, you old fool," Treat snapped.

He reached a hand to his hip, apparently remembered he wasn't packing a gun, and wiped his hand on his pants to cover the gesture.

"I'll be around a while, Treat," Trevannon said quietly. "You won't be. Unless it's pounding leather for thirty and found. Mrs. Carter don't like you. Neither do I, but I'll leave you a choice. Only you'll keep in mind that I'm rodding this outfit, starting now."

"You're a liar!"

Trevannon didn't stir a muscle. "Ask Mrs. Carter."

Treat's swarthy face had shaded down palely at Trevannon's words; now it ruddied with savage feeling. "That's it, eh? Got to the bitch, did you? Big hero-man—"

As he spoke Treat vaulted the bench and started his

plowing lunge around the table to reach Trevannon at its foot. The drifter came to his feet and straddled the bench to meet Treat's rush. The thought flashed across his mind to end this quickly. Near to hand was the heavy coal-oil lamp, off-center of the table toward his end. Trevannon scooped it up and swung full-armed, crashing its base against Treat's bull head. The chimney shattered with the jangling shock and lamp oil sprayed over Treat's face and clothes. Carried on by his own lunge, he crashed headlong into the cold potbellied stove in the corner before plunging on his face. The light stove rocked loosely against the wall, tipped and fell on its side. Disjointed stovepipes clattered down and a black torrent of soot sifted over Treat's inert form.

Trevannon slung his other leg free of the bench and stepped away from it, facing the whole room. "Gentlemen," he said softly, "I do not aim to argue this with any one of you."

"Son," the old man said mildly, "you don't give a man much leeway for argument."

"Not any," Trevannon said flatly. "What's your name?"

"Gabe Morrow, *segundo* here."

The fat cook had waddled in from the kitchen, a cleaver in his hand. He halted, looked down at Bill Treat, and scratched his head foolishly. "Hear you say you're new foreman?"

Trevannon nodded. "Throw some water on him. Where's the wrangler?"

A lean, Indian-looking man grunted. Trevannon glanced at him. "Cut a horse out for Treat. Load him on, with his warsack. If he's got pay coming, get it from Mrs. Carter." His gaze swept the crew and came back to Gabe Morrow. "We'll step outside."

The two men walked off a distance from the bunkhouse before Trevannon asked, "How'd you take your orders, Mr. Morrow?"

"From Kilrain Carter through Treat."

"But you know the routine."

Old Gabe smiled. "I top-handed for some sizable outfits when Bill Treat was in knee-britches. Only there's them thinks when a man passes sixty he loses his grip." His shrewd old eyes glinted. "Kilrain Carter's boots were more'n man-sized, mister."

It was a direct and wholly reasonable challenge; a brief smile flickered Trevannon's lips. "I trail-bossed to New Orleans before the war—for Eli Lapham's Double Bar X in West Texas."

Old Gabe's lips pursed in a soundless whistle. "Heard of the outfit. Hell of a drive, too, that one. You couldn't of been much more'n a kid then." He chuckled. "I didn't ask no question, but you sure as hell answered it."

"I'll answer the other you didn't ask. Man's as good as he proves himself at any age." Trevannon paused deliberately. "I don't know Kaysee or this valley yet. Till I get the feel, I'll need a man to give orders. That man could make my way a lot smoother or a hell of a lot rougher. Got a feeling the men'll follow your lead. How's it to be?"

Old Gabe's shrewd gaze sized the tall, still-faced man before him. "Like the way you sink your stakes, son. Hard, straight. I'll go along."

He extended a hard-calloused hand, and Trevannon took it, saying then, "This homesteader business, Gabe. It sounds like trouble. I want to hear what you think."

"How much you know?" When Trevannon had told him, Gabe Morrow said, "About sums it up. This side of Elk Crick is all patented land. Kil Carter bought out a flock of small outfits years ago. But east of the crick is the big bulk of our graze, and that's all open range. Anyone who's a mind to can homestead over there. That does gravel an oldtimer." Gabe tugged his lower lip embarrassedly. "Still . . . them Canaanites ain't near black as Treat and the Old Man always painted 'em. Either of 'em would of skun us alive if they'd knowed, but fact is the boys and I often dropped in on them people when our work took us over that way. Notwithstandin' that we roughed 'em up that time, even accidentally killed one of their menfolk, those folks're friendly, and forgivin' as all get-out. Make a man plumb ashamed. . . ."

"Was or was not this Bodie Teece a Canaanite?"

Old Gabe's sun-wrinkled face crinkled into a sober frown. "Crazy in the head, that one. Can't judge the rest by him. Good people. Got their odd ways; too Holy Joe for my taste. But what the hell, man's beliefs is his own affair. Still, it's a fact they want a chunk of our open range almighty bad. . . . Look, you want my opinion, here it is: before you do anything else, ride over and talk to old Ephraim Waybeck. He's their leader. Talks over my head, but I cottoned to him."

"I got it," Wes observed dryly, "that this Teece was Waybeck's brother-in-law. Should make me something less than welcome there."

"You don't know Eph Waybeck," Gabe Morrow said quietly. "He'll hear you out and never lift a hand agin you. Take my advice, you'll hear *him* out."

Trevannon scrubbed his stubbled chin with a flat palm, slowly nodded. "All right. I'll do that, Gabe. Now's as good a time as any . . . you give the crew their orders."

"They'll want a time off for the buryin'. No one liked Kilrain Carter much—but every manjack respected him."

"I'll ask Mrs. Carter about that."

Gabe nodded, and Trevannon turned on his heel and headed for the main house. He passed the dark-faced wrangler returning from the house, asked him if he had gotten Treat's pay, and the man gave a bare nod and went on.

As Wes neared the veranda, Andrea Carter stepped out onto it. She was immaculate in a black riding habit with a matching tricorne hat perched on her high-coiled hair. *Colors of the grieving widow,* Trevannon thought ironically, seeing the bright, griefless smile that touched her lips at his approach.

He halted with a foot on the bottom step, touched his hat. "Morning, ma'am."

"Good morning." Andrea's restless gaze wandered to the bunkhouse from which the wrangler had just emerged, helping a stumbling, slack-legged Bill Treat toward the corrals. "Tige Menefee told me. Well, I'm glad *he's* leaving. I suppose when he learned—"

"Yes, ma'am," Wes said dryly, "he didn't like it a little bit. . . . Reckon you'll want town services and a funeral for Mr. Carter?"

"Well," she said uncertainly, "Kilrain was hardly religious. . . ."

"If you like," Trevannon said patiently, "we can bury him here. Might be more fitting. Someone can say a few words. And the crew'll want to attend. Tomorrow be all right?"

She nodded with obvious relief that a problem of irritating decisions was taken off her hands. "I think that will be fine."

He hesitated, weighing his next words. "You'd better hear this, Mrs. Carter. I'm going to ride out to the Canaanite settlement, talk with their head man. Might be we can reach some sort of agreement. Worth a try, to settle any trouble without shooting."

"I—don't think that would be wise."

"You don't," Trevannon murmured with mild irony.

To his surprise, she retorted instantly, "You read people very well, don't you, sir? But you're wrong this time. I meant exactly what I said: *I* don't think it's wise for you to go there alone." Her eyes darkened, lifting toward an empty shed in which Bodie Teece's body lay, covered by a piece of canvas. "Before he shot Kilrain, he said something about learning that Kilrain was in league with—with the Devil. Somebody must have put such a notion in his head."

Trevannon's grave nod was his apology, concealing his startled realization of a fresh side of her many-faceted nature: a mature instinct that was at times aware of her own childish dependency. He told her then what Gabe Morrow had said, and she listened attentively.

"If that is so," she said calmly, "then we certainly should avoid needless violence, if possible. Anyway, you are the general, as well as foreman, here; the decision is yours." Her violet eyes lightened, softened. "But be careful—please."

He nodded, looking away in embarrassment. Whatever her state of mind, she was a damned alluring woman by any standards; her expression could unsettle a man without conveying a hint of boldness that would be unseeming in a newly-made widow.

His gaze absently strayed toward the corrals where Treat now sat his horse, clutching the pommel. His face was slack and sick, but even from here Trevannon could see the naked hate burning in his face. This burly and unwashed man might be a slave to his own lusts, but he had a definite animal cunning, and no man who'd risen to foremanship of Kaysee was incompetent in practical matters. He, Trevannon, had twice beaten and humiliated a brawling bully by cool thinking and faster reflexes, but Treat's cunning and competence, backed by brute strength and his raw pride, made him a dangerous enemy.

The wrangler, after assisting Treat to mount, had gone to the bunkhouse. Now he returned at his flowing, catlike walk, carrying a warsack and a bedroll. He lashed the gear to Treat's saddle. Treat slashed his quirt across his horse's flank with a sudden viciousness. The animal squealed and leaped, and would have knocked Tige Menefee sprawling if he hadn't leaped back with a pantherish quickness. Treat spurred across the yard, his arm flailing up and down, until horse and rider were lost to sight around the far outbuildings.

Andrea released a held breath. "I'm glad he's gone. You hurt him. Now you'll really have to be careful. . . ."

Trevannon nodded, his curious gaze veering back to the wrangler. The man's murky stare had settled on the two of them. It held briefly on Andrea, then found Trevannon with a dead, cold flatness. Menefee's scarred lips twitched. That intensity of look, Trevannon realized, was inspired by his own closeness to the girl. *Why,* he thought amazedly, *the man's crazy jealous. . . .*

Andrea followed his gaze and smiled. "That Tige, such a funny one."

Almost as funny as dying, Trevannon thought grimly, watching the half-breed turn and head back to the corrals where the crew was saddling up. It was like this girl to take a man's affection for granted with a child's thoughtless acceptance of a gift it felt was only its just due. Yet, he realized, in Tige Menefee's case she was safe in doing so; this man's was dumb, selfless adoration of a pure goddess. Only Andrea was no goddess, but a creature of sudden-shifting moods, and Wes had the cold thought: *If she so much as stamped her foot at a man, that Indian would likely kill him.*

Glancing then at the fresh innocence of her face, he felt almost ashamed of the thought. He said, "There any law in this valley?"

"Oh . . ." Andrea tapped the rawhide quirt thonged to her wrist against a smooth cheek, frowning. "You mean we should report Kilrain's death?"

"And Teece's. Sheriff'll find out anyway. Better if he gets it straight from us how it happened. If this thing comes to trouble, best the law has no black marks against us."

"Yes, that's true. Well, the sheriff has his office over in Cedar Wells—that's the county seat. But it's way up on the plateau there"—she pointed westward with the quirt—"not too far as the crow flies, but the escarpment is so high on this side, all the good trails from the valley to the plateau swing way around north—a good two days' ride." Her wonderfully guileless gaze held on him. "By the way, how did you come into the valley?"

"From the south," lied Wes. "Was heading straight through, riding the grubline. Came here by chance."

"Oh. Anyway, there is a deputy sheriff at Coldbrook,

here in the valley. That's Job Bell. I can fetch him, I suppose. . . . I was going for a ride anyhow."

"I'll saddle up for both of us," Trevannon said. "No point putting off that talk with Ephraim Waybeck."

"You don't have to for me," Andrea said smiling. "Tige has my horse all ready, see?"

CHAPTER 7

AS AN AFTERTHOUGHT BEFORE THE CREW LEFT, TREVANNON borrowed a gun and shellbelt from one of them. In spite of Gabe Morrow's optimism, he intended to ride into nothing blind. With like caution, he did not take his bay gelding; he roped out a blaze-face sorrel with the KC brand. Andrea had given him rough directions for reaching the East Bench where the Canaanites had their small settlement. Leaving Kaysee's headquarters, he held due east on its rolling acreage by the sun, which climbed into mid-morning as he rode.

Within an hour he began to hit areas where the rich graze faded to sparseness, and weeds and broad-leaved shrubs had moved in. Here and there the earth was stripped of vegetation, eroded by gullies. Trevannon's brows drew to a fixed scowl as he studied the terrain. The cattle had not been properly scattered here; first, concentrated overgrazing had taken its toll, then numerous sharp hoofs had trampled the grass to extinction . . . and now this area was significantly abandoned.

Wes dismounted by a scalped hillock, squatted down and sifted a handful of the remaining topsoil between his fingers. Loose and sandy, the kind that absorbed a lot of water but didn't hold it. This wasn't farming country, and even grazing should be carefully balanced. Once that topmost layer of virgin sod, accumulated by ages of nonuse, was gone, the undersoil became a plaything for wind and water. He'd seen the disastrous pattern this had followed on the Great Plains. The cattlemen started the process; the plowmen finished it. Drought and dust followed, and abandoned ranches and farms.

Trevannon had worked cattle all his life, but he was honest enough to admit that if the sodbusters were the worst offenders, it was only by chance; his own kind was equally blind. Only a few alert men appeared concerned about the long-range effects of the prodigal waste left by the white man in his westward rape of the continent. John Wesley Powell, a government geologist, had recorded an outline of the process, what must be done now if the Western lands were to be saved from the disaster that would come, but Powell's findings were gathering dust in Congressional archives. So Trevannon had heard. But the vast majority, he knew, were greedy enough to say, in effect, to hell with the future. . . .

Still it was a cattleman's gorge of anger that now rose hot and angry in Trevannon's chest. After talking with Gabe Morrow he'd felt strong doubts about the rightness of Kaysee's position, and now knew in a cold corner of his mind the unfairness of this sudden partisan feeling. Though this country should be restricted to grazing, Kaysee had itself misused the land. Yet an uncompromising half-hostility seeded in his mind, as he rode on across heightening land, ridge-broken and dotted with timber stands.

It was in this mood that he topped a ridge and faced across the wide-sweeping Bench where a nucleus of many farm buildings centered a vast swath of tilled fields. The worst of his expectations were fulfilled as he frowned across the scraggly plots of corn and beans. Nearly harvest time, and damned poor returns there'd be. As usual too, the damned sodbusters had indiscriminately felled trees that would have broken the soil-tearing winds and provided moisture-storing roots. He put the sorrel down the slope till he hit some wagon ruts between two fields, followed these toward the buildings.

A man who was hoeing out weeds between pathetic corn

rows near the roadside looked up, removed his hat and sleeved his forehead. He wore linsey-woolsey homespuns of a drab neutral color.

Trevannon cantered the sorrel to a halt as the man, with a pleasant smile and nod, said, "Morning, neighbor."

Trevannon nodded, saying shortly, "Where can I find Ephraim Waybeck?"

Apparently unaffected by a grim response, the man said affably, "First house to your right. But here, friend . . . you look hot and dry—" He tramped over to a waterjug sitting in the tall grass by the road.

Trevannon abruptly put the gelding into motion, throwing a curt, "No thanks," over his shoulder. By the time he reached the first house, he was enough ashamed of his rudeness to grin down at the small boy who was building a mud castle in the yard.

"Hi there, carpenter. Is this where Mr. Waybeck lives?"

"I am Ephraim Waybeck."

The voice was deep and gentle, and Trevannon lifted his gaze to its owner, seeing a man tall as himself now descending the rickety stoop to cross the yard. He was old, yet walked with a swinging, youthful stride. Trevannon couldn't help the awed fascination he felt at this barrel-chested man, who had a muscled, fatless girth of body to match his height, and a mane of hair that flowed into the great snowy beard spilling over his chest like fresh hoar-frost. His blue eyes seemed to burn from gentleness to fiery fervor and back again, yet always mirroring a great, calm certainty. An Old Testament patriarch, Trevannon thought, stepped from a bygone age. . . .

"Come down, sir, come down. You look hot and thirsty." His white brows flew together in a stormy frown. "You passed Elia in the fields; didn't he offer you a drink?"

Trevannon nodded reservedly, instinctively holding himself on guard against the warm, tremendous magnetism of the man.

Ephraim Waybeck studied his face a moment as though

reading his thoughts; the quick eyes suddenly twinkled. "I see. But of course you'll rest and sup with us . . . I beg you." With his last words came the faint and rueful smile of a man who knew that even his invitations sounded like commands.

Wes swung to the ground, glancing at the tow-headed boy. He was about ten and he was eyeing the gun at Trevannon's hip with grave fascination.

"Jerry," Ephraim Waybeck said sharply, and the boy jerked from his trance.

"Yes, Grandpa."

"Take the gentleman's horse to the stable; water and grain it. See you take care now; the animal looks heated. . . . We'll go inside now, sir. Your pleasure is ours, Mister—?"

"Trevannon, Wesley Trevannon."

He braced his hand to meet this venerable giant's clasp, but Waybeck's horny hand was as gentle as it was firm. They crossed the yard to the house, which was more like an oversize lean-to shack. It was unpainted, with not even a tarpaper layer to cover the warped and weathered sheathing. This retempered his mood to cold disapproval. *The usual damn nester's sloppiness*, he thought.

Noting his bleak study, old Ephraim said gently, "Paint and trim, sir, are vanity of vanities."

"And humble pie is hell on good lumber," Trevannon growled under his breath; Ephraim, hearing the tone if not the words, only smiled. . . .

They stepped into a single large room that was combination kitchen, parlor and dining room, with wooden double bunks at either end. The hand-carved furniture was crude and meager. An elderly woman moved slowly back and forth in a rocking chair, a large Bible spread open on her knees. Her gaze was distantly vacant in a thin face with its tightly bound frame of silvery hair.

"My wife, sir," said Ephraim Waybeck, his deep voice very gentle. "This is Mister Trevannon, Mother. He'll stay for dinner. . . ."

The old woman's eyes riveted, as had the boy's, on Trevannon's holstered Colt. Her thin fingers trembled on the Book; a little moan left her tight and bloodless lips. Ephraim Waybeck's hand dropped lightly to her shoulder, an infinite sadness and affection in the gesture that made Trevannon look uneasily away.

Through the heavy steam and cooking odors that filled the room he now saw another woman bent down by a fieldstone fireplace. Food utensils were set on the glowing embers, and a large iron pot hung from an iron rod set in the stones. The woman was stirring a stew with a long-handled ladle, and though she was stooping with back turned, Trevannon knew that she was young.

Waybeck raised his voice. "Calla, come meet our guest . . . my daughter-in-law, Mr. Trevannon. You've met her son—which completes immediate introductions."

The young woman wiped her hands on her ragged apron, crossed the room with a quick trim stride. Her finely molded face and strong, full-breasted body were scarcely marked by the hard drudgery that was plainly her lot, though he judged her age as not quite thirty. Her fair hair was drawn to a prim knot at the back of her head. Her eyes, of a dark, clear gray, held Trevannon's attention. They mirrored a serene and full acceptance of life that awed him, the same iron-gentle quality he'd felt in Ephraim. Yet Calla Waybeck's smile was quick and shy, and she hesitantly moved her right hand upward and then dropped it. Trevannon put out his hand and held it there till she took it, and her smile warmed.

Trevannon caught himself grinning; he forced his mouth to a sober line, said formally, "How do you do?"

With a pleased chuckle, Ephraim Waybeck boomed, "Is the food ready, Calla . . . and a pitcher of cold water for our guest?"

She nodded, still smiling, and bustled back and forth between the fireplace and the crude puncheon table. Ephraim assisted his wife to a bench on one side. The old woman moved very slowly and stiffly, hardly taking her eyes off the stranger, rather, his gun. Trevannon skirted the table, taking the opposite bench where he could face the door. He waited till Calla had summoned Jerry and the family was seated, old Ephraim at the head, before sliding onto the bench beside the boy.

Trevannon half-reached for the pitcher of water, withdrew his hand as he saw the family bowing their heads, and sat stiffly through old Waybeck's lengthy grace. But he did listen. Remembering the rote-droned and hellfire prayers and sermons he'd heard as a boy, he contrasted them to the simple, moving speech of this man. Ephraim Waybeck was plainly a man full of the love of the earth and the things known by the earth, and this feeling chorded powerfully through his words of thanks.

Finished, Ephraim at once reached for the dish of stew and ladled a generous portion onto his guest's plate. He cocked a brow as he served, saying mildly, "A cowman such as you obviously are could only be among us on business, sir; but I trust you'll wait till we've eaten? Too, if you'll yield an old man the privilege of bluntness, a visitor of relaxed suspicion would not so hastily have chosen a seat facing the door."

Trevannon felt embarrassed heat rise to his face. "That's right." He hesitated, added, "Your son won't be joining us?"

"My son James—my only son—has been dead these many months," Ephraim Waybeck said quietly. Trevannon glanced quickly at Calla, saw her hands still momentarily on a dish. She drew a quick breath, then reached the dish across to her son, her face wholly composed.

"The only family member not present is my wife's brother, Bodiah Teece. He has been gone several days, not unusual as he travels always on foot. He is," Ephraim added wryly, "something of a preacher."

A mouthful of stew soured on Trevannon; he swallowed with an effort. He'd half-forgotten, in the warm hospitality here, the little fanatic who had died by his hand. He could not go on with this; better to have it out now. He cleared his throat to speak, shifting his weight on the bench. His holstered gun bumped loudly against the bench. The old woman jerked sharply at the sound, lifted her head and fixed on his face with a terribly intensity. Her lips moved almost soundlessly, yet he caught the words clearly:

"And another horse came forth, a red horse: and to him that sat thereon it was given to take peace from the earth, and that they should slay one another: and there was given to him a great sword. . . ."

Ephraim Waybeck got up and came around the table, helped his wife slowly to her feet. "Come, Mother . . . you'd best lie down."

As docile as a child, the old woman permitted herself to be led to one of the bunks. Ephraim eased her back on the blankets, touched her face lightly with a great hand, and the tension seemed to flow from her. She relaxed, hands folded on her breast, and stared vacantly upward.

Calla Waybeck leaned forward, saying softly, "We don't apologize for my mother-in-law, Mr. Trevannon. She is not responsible . . . her mind has not been right since Jim was killed."

"Killed?"

"Yes. Evidently you're a stranger to the valley, or you'd have heard the story. When we first came here, we filed our homesteads on land claimed by the Kaysee ranch. Legally it was public domain—but one night their riders raided us, burned our dwellings one by one, and drove us all, men, women and children, toward this Bench—herding us like beasts. Violent resistance is against our teachings . . . but Jim—my husband—lost his temper. He dragged one of the riders from his saddle . . . another shot him. He lived for a week in pain and delirium. His mother watched it all, never leaving his side—but she could not save him. She was never a strong woman, and it left her as you see her. . . ."

Ephraim Waybeck took his seat again, and Trevannon gave him a sharp glance. "Let 'em get away with it, eh?"

"Sir," Ephraim said softly, "our creed is simple but firm. As we hold the hereafter to be an unanswerable mystery, we emphasize rather peace among men and the good life on this earth."

"Peace," Trevannon said harshly. "Much peace you'll find in this world. . . ."

Ephraim smiled sadly. "Indeed, at times it has seemed so. . . . In Ohio, I was a common farmer, though with an advantage of considerable formal education, a man as venial, lusting, and profane as any. Then, a few years ago, I felt the Command . . . directing me to take my household and such friends as would follow me and seek a new country where we might abide in peace and friendship and live that which we professed. Like Israel of old we set our faces toward the wilderness and sought Canaan. Hence our name—the Canaanites. It is not important, except to give us a sense of solidarity. A long search led us to this valley, and again came the Command, clear and unmistakable. This is our home; we shall not be driven from it. Yet, we're farmers, and this Bench is poor land; that claimed by Kaysee ranch is rich. As we cannot meet force with force, it seems we must wait . . . hope that God and time will soften Kilrain Carter's heart."

Trevannon scowled. "I don't get it. As government homesteaders, you're entitled to government protection. All you had to do was get the sheriff to send for a U.S. Marshal or a Land Office agent. . . ."

Ephraim said steadily, "Our sanction to that land is not by the word of man, but by a law far higher. We will observe man-made laws, but we do not appeal to them. To force ethical behavior upon others is wrong; moreover, to appeal to such law would be to show a tragic weakness of faith. Our good friend the lawyer McQuayle who recommended the land we homesteaded did not approve of my stand in this—but so it must be."

Trevannon said slowly, "That's why you didn't take the murder of your son to the sheriff—why you didn't try to—"

"Avenge his death? God knows I had the impulse; I wanted to seek out Kilrain Carter—but I restrained myself. And sought God's help . . . to find a reason."

Trevannon started to shake his head in resignation, then

checked the gesture. But Ephraim caught it; a tolerant light sparkled in his eyes. "I hardly expected a miracle, Mr. Trevannon. But the answer came in my heart—wait, be patient."

Their religion, Trevannon thought sardonically. Even to a uniform: the drab, linsey-woolsey dresses and identical prim hairdos of the women; the similar frayed and oft-patched shirts and trousers and round-crowned black hats worn by the men and boys. But inward ridicule couldn't still the sense of awe he knew before the tremendous serenity and quiet happiness of these people, making itself felt through the sense of tragedy that lingered over this household.

"Mr. Waybeck," he said uneasily, "there's a thing you'll have to hear. In private."

Ephraim gave the barely touched food a glance, nodded. "Something in your tone suggests that it cannot wait. Come then, we'll step outside."

They stood up and Wes preceded Ephraim Waybeck, both men ducking their lofty heights beneath the low lintel. Trevannon paced off from the house a half-dozen yards, swung to face Ephraim Waybeck.

"Your brother-in-law, Bodie Teece, won't be coming back. He's dead. That's part of what I came to tell you."

"Ah, Lord. . . ." Ephraim raised a stunned hand, dropped it helplessly. "I had thought Bodiah's madness to be a harmless thing . . . and now this. What happened?"

Trevannon spoke for five minutes, and Ephraim Waybeck's expression did not alter, except for a deepening sadness. At last he said, "Little wonder that you faced the door, held yourself tensely as though among enemies . . . but you had nothing to fear, son."

"Know that now."

Ephraim turned his head to stare across the parched fields, musing aloud. "My teachings became, in Bodiah, a malignant obsession. He perverted my central doctrine, evangelized it with the savor of brimstone. My teachings were never to be exhorted by such means. . . . We'll send a wagon to Kaysee for Bodiah's body. I will tell my wife he met his death by accident; a lie will be kindest. Perhaps he has found peace. Kilrain Carter too. . . ."

Trevannon toed at a clod of earth, said nothing.

"You did what had to be done," Ephraim said gently, "to save that young woman's life." His voice gained a brisk note. "There's another thing you came to tell me?"

Trevannon drew a deep breath, let it out. "I'm the new foreman of Kaysee."

"I see. . . . Mr. Trevannon, coming here as you did was very difficult for you—a very fine thing."

"You may not think so when you hear the rest."

"Perhaps then you've come to renew Kilrain Carter's old ultimatum to us . . . to stay off the land your ranch claims?"

"Look," Trevannon said roughly, "I'm not unreasonable. This isn't farming country, Mr. Waybeck. The soil's bad, the growing season's way too short in this high-up country. Start plowing it up, you'll only ruin it for everyone." He shook his head impatiently as Ephraim started to reply. "I heard your argument, the Lord's willed it you settle here. I don't know about things like that. Me, I just know cattle; I know the land. I think you got that feeling, maybe in a different way. And you got to understand one thing—you can't farm this valley."

"But we cannot leave," Ephraim declared passionately.

"Look . . . why crop the land? Other valley people raise cattle."

"You mean—change an entire way of life to which all of us here were born?" Ephraim shook his shaggy head—yet with indecision. "I do not know. This would take time, and pain."

"Sir," Wes said softly, "I'm almighty hopeful you make the right choice. There's times when faith and good intentions just ain't enough. There's plain facts, too. One of which is that for you to plow up Kaysee range would be a damnfool and wasteful thing—and if you try it, I'll stop you."

"You butcher."

Calla Waybeck's voice struck out with a controlled passion that was startling. Trevannon looked around, saw her standing in the doorway with her hands on little Jerry's shoulders, hugging him against her skirt.

"Haven't you done enough?" she whispered. "You and your kind . . . you murdered this boy's father, put his grandmother out of her mind. And so easily propose to do the same thing again. But why wait?" She pushed the boy forward a step. "Here he is. You have a gun. Finish your dirty work, Mr. Trevannon! Nobody will try to stop you; it's against our—"

"Calla." Old Ephraim spoke very quietly, no less firmly for that. "Why don't you clear the table?"

She stood proud and straight, her eyes blazing. But she said nothing, only stepped back inside, pulling her son with her. A moment later there was an angry clatter of dishes.

"Another point of my belief," Ephraim murmured, "is that our evil impulses are part of us, with the good. Better to turn the bad energy into useful work. Which is the reason for our lack of what folk regard as necessary comfort. We keep poor and busy—and out of mischief's way." A faint smile touched his bearded lips. "Calla does not take kindly to some of my beliefs. Certainly she has never forgiven her husband's unpunished murder. For all her quiet ways, she's a strong-minded woman, and when she marries again, I think it will be outside of our group." He paused thoughtfully. "Actually she's quite like you, Mr. Trevannon."

"Me?"

"Why, yes. I should say that you are one of those rare and fortunate people who carry their religion about as a part of them. With your obvious courage and principles, I've sensed also a self-reliance that is not arrogance, but only a great completeness as natural to you as breathing. You are not, I think, wholly at peace with yourself, but there is another reason for that." His white brows climbed a notch. "Sometimes a man needs someone else—"

"I'll be going," Trevannon growled. "And Mr. Waybeck, I meant what I said. You think it over, think on it hard. Make the right choice, I'll do what I can for you."

"You've given me much food for thought." Ephraim sighed profoundly. "Now give me a little time. . . ."

"All you want. But no Kaysee range for plowing."

"Come again, my friend. Soon." With this farewell, old Waybeck turned back toward the house, slowly shaking his head.

Wes got his horse from the little stable behind the house, cantered across the yard and swung down the road. Then he heard young Mrs. Waybeck call, "Wait . . . wait a minute, please."

She came swiftly across the yard, holding her skirts, stopped breathlessly by his stirrup and pushed a fine wisp of fair hair back from her forehead. "I'm sorry," she said simply. "You're not like that other Kaysee foreman. A fool could see that."

Trevannon nodded acceptance of the apology, said shortly, "Bill Treat's already through at Kaysee." Hesitating, he then added, "I didn't say it, but I was sorry too. About Bodie Teece."

"Yes, I heard that part. Forgive me for listening. So little news comes to us here." Calla Waybeck paused, frowning lightly. "What I don't understand is what drove Uncle Bodie . . . to do what he did. He was not a man who was easy to know, and he was rarely home. . . . I—I can't say that his death truly touches me. But I could have sworn that he was harmless—for all his bluster. Something we didn't know about must have driven him. . . ."

Trevannon leaned forward, crossing his arms on his pommel. "That seems to be the general opinion. . . . Mrs. Waybeck, there's a name that keeps cropping up in this affair: Cassius McQuayle. Like to hear your opinion of him. He have an ax to grind?"

"Why, Grandpa Ephraim considers Mr. McQuayle our great friend. And he does seem a kindly, grandfatherly sort of man—yet . . . somehow, I always felt he was almost too good to be true. He talks of justice, of the rights of the downtrodden. But I'll never forget how he looked when Grandpa refused to file charges against Kaysee, after those cowboys drove us from our homestead claims. He'd been strangely insistent that we settle where *he* told us . . . that once, at least, he seemed to wear a different face . . . an ugly one."

Trevannon smiled gravely. "Woman's got a knack for sizing up such things. Still, by my lights, McQuayle was right. A man should fight for what's his."

"My husband—did." A bitter remembering darkened Calla Waybeck's eyes. "At least I can tell Jerry that his father died like a man, defending his family and home."

Trevannon was silent to this plain renunciation of Ephraim Waybeck's pacifistic stand. Ephraim, he reflected, had shown his people how to live with simple goodness and charity in a dog-eat-dog society . . . but in the world as it was, such people inevitably suffered. Calla had too much sharp spirit not to revolt against that fact; he liked her better for it. His gaze lifted to the boy Jerry who was standing in the yard, toeing at the earth while he regarded the man on horseback with childhood's wondering reserve.

"Kid's too old to be building mud houses," Wes observed.

"He should be with a father now," Calla agreed. "Hunting, perhaps. But Grandpa Ephraim permits no guns to be kept here." She added smilingly, "You like children, Mr. Trevannon."

"My boy would have been about his age," Wes said musingly. "I guess—"

"Oh . . . you had a family?"

"A wife. Son. Dead now. Typhus."

"And I prattled of my troubles," she said softly. "Again—I'm sorry."

Trevannon shrugged brusquely, straightened in the saddle and caught up his reins. "I'll be going. One thing I wish you'd do . . . tell me where it was on Kaysee range you made your homesteading try. I'd like to ride there and look it over."

"Gladly." She stepped back from his stirrup, studying his face in her quiet way. "Grandpa Ephraim asked you to come again. Will you?"

Wes hesitated, in that moment felt something electric pass between their locked glances. He couldn't deny the way he'd felt drawn to this woman from first sight, and yet he was baffled. *You could make too much out of this,* he warned himself, and then said in a neutral tone, "Yes'm. I'll want to hear what he decides to do."

CHAPTER 8

THE TOWN OF COLDBROOK WAS NO MORE THAN A FEW weathered frame buildings sprawling slapdash on either side of a wagon-rutted trail in a creek-bend of the lower valley. Its only excuse for being was a supply center for Kaysee and the smaller valley outfits; goods were freighted in monthly from Cedar Wells, the county seat. Kilrain Carter, as the valley's first settler, had set up the general trade store to service his ranch hands, and later a couple of saloons, a feed company, a blacksmith shop, a hotel, and a professional building had grown up around it.

At high noon Bill Treat sat on the porch of the small Coldbrook Hotel, his loafer's chair back-tilted against the building's clapboarded front. Picking his teeth after a meal in the hotel dining room, a meal which he'd barely tasted.

Seven good years as foreman of a great ranch . . . shot to hell. The best damned ramrod in the territory booted out of his job as casually as you'd snap your fingers. He couldn't quite believe it still. Kaysee had become Treat's life. The stolid routine of his job suited his nature; the tough authority of it was an obsessive need in him. At first a dozen wild schemes for regaining his post had swarmed in his mind, but the hopeless futility of each was soon apparent. Now he felt empty and a little sick, wondering where he could go from here and not really caring.

He was sure of one thing: a cold hatred of Trevannon that

cankered in him so strongly he could taste it. He gingerly rubbed the base of his thick neck where Trevannon had clubbed him with the lamp. Paying Trevannon back was a thing he could damned definitely do. Catch the drifter alone, nail him from ambush, bury the body in a ravine where it would never be found. With Trevannon out of the way, he might even regain his old job.

Yet it was risky, damned risky. If Trevannon suddenly disappeared, suspicion would logically center on Bill Treat. Even though nothing could be proved without a body, murder was an appalling step . . . especially inside the jurisdiction of that law-leech Sheriff Vandermeer. Treat's younger, wilder days were past; the caution of an older man warned him to consider every angle carefully. . . .

He drew a cheap cigar from his vest pocket, snapped a match alight on his thumbnail, touched it to his cigar and tossed the wisp-furling match away. His eyes narrowed against the smoke as he saw a woman on horseback swing onto the street and dismount by the jail. It was Andrea Carter. He leaned forward, elbows on his thighs as he watched her graceful motions of dismounting, feeling the hungry frustration that boiled in him at every sight of her. That simple little bitch parading in front of his eyes daily always set up this crazy gnawing in his guts. Acting so damned high and untouchable. Too good for him . . . *like hell she is!* Still, she was a lost cause as far as he was concerned, he admitted bitterly.

She entered the jail where its office fronted on the street—probably to report her husband's killing to Bell, the deputy sheriff. In about five minutes, she emerged, Job Bell at her heels looking red-faced and flustered as he assisted her to her sidesaddle. Treat, with cynical insight and dour amusement, guessed that the young deputy, who'd always had a serious case on Kilrain Carter's beautiful bride, was already seeing a chance for himself with the freshly widowed girl and was remorsefully ashamed of the thought.

Bell went downstreet to the livery stable, giving Treat a bare nod in passing, and shortly rode out on his horse, joined Andrea and the two of them jogged out of town. Bell probably planned to question the Canaanites, Treat thought cynically; it was damned well certain that he'd get no satisfaction from them. If they did know why Bodie Teece had been driven from empty threats against Kilrain Carter to a killing, they'd say nothing, hanging together like leeches as always. . . .

Treat glanced idly toward the north end of town. Tensed in his chair as he recognized the hulking, bear-huge man astride a paint horse just riding in. *Well, I'm damned. Jans Vandermeer. What brings him down here?*

Curious, Treat lounged to his feet and stepped to the edge of the porch, leaning his shoulder against a gallery post. He lazily hailed the sheriff as he came abreast of the hotel.

"How, Dutchy."

"Hello, Bill."

Vandermeer paced his mount sideward to the hotel steps, then removed his dusty hat and produced a handkerchief. He ran it around the sweatband of his hat, passed it over his pale, sweat-matted hair. He did this methodically, then glanced up at Treat with a broad, ruddy face crinkled by the friendly smile that never reached his cold, china-blue eyes. Eyes that never relaxed their chill alertness, mirroring the dogged, single-minded patience of a career that also was Vandermeer's religion: catching lawbreakers.

"So now," the sheriff chided mildly, "the foreman of Kaysee loafs in town on a weekday. It is not like you, Bill."

Treat grunted. "Off-pasture yourself, ain't you? You generally make the rounds of the county towns once a month. Wasn't you down here just a week ago?—Hoss looks like you been pushing hard."

Vandermeer gave a slow and ponderous nod, saddle leather creaking with a shift of his massive weight, of which hardly an ounce was fat. "Yesterday the bank in Cedar

Wells was robbed. Two men, both masked. With a posse I trailed them on the ridge running south from town."

"Huh. How much they get?"

"Twenty thousand and odd dollars, Bill."

Treat whistled.

"Considerable loot, eh? They must have quarreled over it, for we found the body of one in a thicket by the ridge trail. Shot through the heart. The other we followed to the eastern edge of the plateau, where he eluded us by plunging his horse into a wash swollen by the storm. We were not foolhardy enough to follow, judging that he would drown. My posse returned to Cedar Wells, but I stayed."

Treat grinned. "Yeah, *you'd* want to be sure."

Another heavy, humorless nod. "Yes. When the storm passed, and the water had died to a trickle, I entered the wash and followed it down through the terraces to the bottom. I found no body. But this—" The sheriff's hamlike hand dipped into a saddlebag; he held up a cedar-butted Colt's. "His gun. He somehow lost it in the gully. But made his way safely to the base of the plateau and this valley of yours. I spent till dark looking for sign, but the rain had wiped out his trail. I camped the night and searched again this morning, again found nothing. So I rode to Coldbrook to enlist the help of Deputy Bell. If the robber is still in the valley, we must find him." His glacial-blue gaze studied Treat. "If he continued to head east, he might have come to Kaysee headquarters. I thought perhaps you might have seen him, Bill."

Treat's mind had skipped with immediate suspicion to Trevannon, ferreting out the possibilities with a rising excitement. *By God, it might be!* He rubbed his chin, saying slowly, "Well, now, hard to say. There *was* a saddle bum rode into Kaysee late yesterday, named of Wes Trevannon—"

"Did he ride a bay gelding horse?" Vandermeer demanded swiftly. "Did he wear a gun—or not?"

"Hold your horses, Dutchy," Treat said. "Wait'll you hear the rest of it. . . ." He launched into his narrative rapidly; the sheriff listened in a mounting amazement he couldn't quite hide.

When Treat had finished, Vandermeer said gently, "That is my man for sure. A bay gelding horse. And he wore no gun, eh? What is greatly surprising to me is that a man of this stripe risks his life to save Ms. Carter from that little madman."

Treat shrugged. "Dunno about that. Hellfire, though, man's one smooth talker, that's sure . . . he talked Miz Carter into firing me, puttin' him in as foreman. Seems he's one of them there confidence men. O' course, Miz Carter was grateful to him and all—but I put in a lot of good years for old Kilrain. Man, man; don't seem nohow fair. . . ."

Vandermeer nodded thoughtfully. "It is hard to believe that Kilrain Carter is gone. He was like part of the land itself." He added with token sympathy, "A cruel break for you, Bill."

Treat drew on his cigar, frowning at its tip. "I'm a direct man, Dutchy. A woman favors them smooth talkers." He paused momentarily. "Look, you riding out to arrest this Trevannon?"

"I will talk to the man, you may be sure."

"Couldn't make it stick, eh?"

"This is doubtful," Vandermeer admitted. "He was masked, and so the clerks of the bank did not see his face. And of course he has probably hidden the money by now. I am sure this man is our guilty one, but our courts proceed on the assumption of a man's innocence. It is for the prosecution to prove guilt. And this is very little proof, Bill—the horse, the lost gun which I cannot show is his, the time of his providential arrival at Kaysee. Thinly circumstantial, do you see?"

"Suppose," Treat said gently, "you could turn up the twenty thousand. It figures he's hid it by now. You'd likely find it on Kaysee headquarters or close by. . . ."

Vandermeer smiled grimly. "The money found on Kay-see, where only one arrival, Trevannon, could have brought it, should be very convincing to any judge and jury. But shall we then overturn every square foot of earth on the ranch?"

"No. But look, Dutchy. Suppose you hold off on the arrest. Sort of lull his suspicions. Meantime I'll ride back to Kaysee and hire on. Trevannon offered me a job on the crew. Tell him I changed my mind, I'll take it. Then I'll scout around, scour every likely place. Know that spread like the palm o' my hand. There's a good chance I could turn up the loot. If I do"—he spread his hands—"you can take your man on a charge that'll stick."

"That is good thinking, and a most generous offer, Bill."

"For strictly selfish reasons, Dutchy. I want my old job."

Vandermeer returned Treat's wide grin. "That is so. Good. You go on to Kaysee, Bill, and I will stay with Deputy Bell in town till you bring me word of success or of failure. . . ."

"Bell, he left town just before you rode in. Miz Carter fetched him. Reckon he's out investigatin' the killin's."

Vandermeer said approvingly, "Young Bell has the makings of a good officer. I will wait at the jail for his return. And I will be waiting on news from you."

He raised a hand in parting, cantered his mount toward the livery stable, and Treat watched him go, narrow eyes burning with satisfaction. His shoulders shook with silent laughter. He was pretty certain that his old position would be returned if he were to appeal to Andrea Carter's mother rather than the girl. Mrs. Congreve would have the sense to see that only he, with Trevannon out of the running, could fill the foremanship of Kaysee.

Best of all, a robber convicted of so sizable a theft should collect a lengthy sentence. A bullet from ambush would mean too easy, too quick a death for the man he hated. A proud, independent hardcase like Trevannon would die slowly behind prison walls. Treat's cigar had gone cold, and he snapped another match alight to fire it up. But an exultant chuckle escaped him, and the explosion of breath blew out the match.

CHAPTER 9

On HIS WAY BACK TO KAYSEE, TREVANNON SWUNG WIDE TO the north to see for himself the tract of land recommended by Cassius McQuayle to his Canaanite friends. Following Calla Waybeck's directions, he found it easily, a pocket of bottom land easily comprising two sections along the northeast boundary. The many-branched creek that supplied fertility to Kaysee's sprawling acreage cut through it running north and south. Trevannon halted the sorrel on a rise and studied it over. It was a typical chunk of rangeland with no more to recommend it for money crops than the rest of this cattle valley. From here he could pick out the charred remains that marked one homestead of the Canaanites' aborted claims.

What, he wondered, was this lawyer McQuayle's angle? Bill Treat had thought the man had one, a possibility echoed by Calla Waybeck. Why should the lawyer have been insistent about the Canaanites' filing on this particular parcel of land, apparently no different, better or worse, than any other quarter section on this vast, grass-covered valley floor? Was McQuayle beating some private drum? Only one man could answer this, and Wes grimly resolved to call on Cassius McQuayle soon. A peaceful settlement of this range feud could be undermined by someone working in the background for his own hidden reasons. If someone had really incited Bodie Teece to facilitate the seizing of this land, it surely hadn't been the Canaanites themselves, he was now certain.

Pondering, Trevannon turned the sorrel southeast toward Kaysee headquarters, following a creek tributary. An hour later he hauled up to let his horse drink from the rushing brook. His keen-ranging eyes idly quested the wind-rippled grass. Halted and tensed on a black dot moving across the neutral greens and tans of this flat plain. He had to squint to make out a horse with its rider crouched against its mane. A runaway. A second rider pounded behind, evidently trying to overtake it. But the far-stretching gait of the first animal held an easy lead.

The runaway was angling generally his way, so Trevannon set the sorrel to an unhurried lope to head it off. Coming nearer, he felt a thin shock of recognition. This was the big black he'd seen Tige Menefee saddle for Andrea Carter that morning. And now he made out the girl's face, white with exultance rather than fear, he thought, then knew he must be mistaken. The black was out of control; a fall at this pace could kill her.

Trevannon started to rein around hard, spurring to bring his horse into stride with Andrea's so he could grab her rein. Then the black plunged sideward into a ground dip; its hoofs flailed away its footing, and momentum sent it into a skidding plunge on its side. Andrea was thrown clear of her sidesaddle, rolling to a stop a couple of yards away.

Trevannon pulled up the sorrel and left his saddle, running as his feet hit the ground. She was already sitting up when he reached her side. Her little hat sat askew on the broken tumble of her hair, one cheek smudged and skinned. She rubbed her nose with a grubby palm, giving him a gaminlike grin, and extended her hand. He pulled her to her feet, thinking unbelievingly, *She started that crazy run apurpose!*

The second rider thundered to a halt, threw himself from horseback, breathing heavily. Andrea met the heavy disapproval in their looks with a little frown. "Well, really, can't a girl have any fun?"

"Wonder you weren't killed!" the youth gasped. Trevannon now noted the star glinting above his shirt pocket. He wasn't over twenty-one, a lean and wiry youth with a blond cowlick, not yet filled out by maturity . . . or, Trevannon guessed, by experience.

Andrea, her face gay and flushed, said, "Job Bell, deputy sheriff . . . Mr. Trevannon, new Kaysee foreman."

Young Bell didn't offer to shake hands. He gave Andrea a brief, sultry glance before fixing his attention on Trevannon. His fists flexed once; a dark scowl muddied his stare. Another of her jealous victims, Trevannon knew wearily . . . Treat, Menefee, and now Job Bell. Each with his own brand of lust, devotion, or romantic dreams revolving around this widowed girl who'd been molded into a neat and attractive package of woman purged of every womanly feeling.

"We just came from Kaysee," Bell announced. "I looked at the bodies. Seems to have happened as Mrs. Carter said."

"That mean I pass?" Trevannon murmured.

Job Bell flushed. "No offense," he said coldly. "My job. You're a stranger, mister. A double murder—killing," he amended without haste, "isn't so usual."

"To say the least," Trevannon agreed soberly. "Heading out to question the Canaanites now, are you?"

"Seems sensible. I talked to Mrs. Carter's mother; she thinks they may have goaded Teece into attacking Mr. Carter." He gave Trevannon a narrow regard. "Mrs. Carter says you had intended riding out to see them?"

Wes inclined his head briefly. "I have."

Bell said with obvious reluctance, "And your opinion?"

"That they're poor and honest people trying like the devil to mind their own business."

"There was Bodie Teece, though," Bell observed with a thin, triumphant smile.

"Exception that proves the rule. I won't try to advise you, Mr. Bell." Because Bell's smug, surly manner was irritating, Trevannon added, "Man should be entirely free to make his own mistakes."

Bell grated his teeth, a trick Trevannon guessed he'd developed to master a quick-flaring temper. "That's right," Bell snapped. "Except I reserve one piece of advice for nosy greenhorns: let the law handle its own mad dogs. We don't need help!"

"Why, certainly," Trevannon agreed gravely. He touched his hat to Andrea and started to rein past them.

"Wait a bit, Wes," Andrea said brightly. "It was a very nice ride, Job. But I must go home now." A scowl flicked Bell's face, and she smiled sweetly. "It's a long ride to the Canaanites', Job. You won't be starting back before nightfall. Propriety, you know . . ."

Propriety! Trevannon nearly snorted aloud . . . one day a widow, and she was playing fire between men with a little-girl coquetry. If a couple of more killings didn't come out of this, it would be a damned miracle. . . .

Job Bell swallowed hard, fashioned a weak grin. "Sure. That's right. Well, be seeing you." To Trevannon he gave a totally unfriendly nod, mounted up and spurred savagely across the shallow creek and eastward.

Trevannon set his horse apace alongside the girl's, and they rode in silence. Aware of her frank, intent sideglances at him, he grimly said nothing. Andrea was used to men's attentions. When she at last spoke, a faint pique marred her tone.

"I think it's marvelous how you've taken hold at the ranch." She seemed to linger thoughtfully on that casual remark. "In some ways, you're very like Kilrain—was."

He didn't reply.

"Oh, I don't mean outwardly," she went on obliviously, caught up in this notion as with a new toy. "Even in manner, you're very different. But I feel that same sense of *strength*, do you know?"

"Job there, now," Trevannon deliberately veered the subject, "he don't look like any kind of weakling."

"Physically, of course not," she said impatiently, "but Job and I practically grew up together. His father was the former deputy in Coldbrook. When he retired, Job sort of succeeded him. But honestly—Job is still a *boy!*"

To that Trevannon carefully said nothing, and there was another silence. Andrea's profile was a cameo of restless discontent as they reached a point at which the creek suddenly broadened into a wide bowl. Here the water gathered deep and placid before taking up its narrow course again.

Andrea abruptly halted her black on the grassy bank, staring across the wind-riffled pond surface where sunlight caught as fractured chains of mobile gold.

Wes broke the silence. "It looks deep."

"It's deep enough," she said. "Dark and deep." Her teeth caught her lower lip; she shivered, though hot sunlight westered against their backs.

"Goose walk over your grave?"

Her glance was quick and dark. "Why did you say that?"

Wes shrugged. Her gaze dragged back to the pool in brooding fascination, voice toneless and low as though she'd retreated far into herself. "We used to steal off from town on hot summer days when we were children. Job and I. It was a long ride, but there was no other place we could swim. The water was always cold, no matter what the weather. Job tried to dive to the bottom once. He was under a long time. And he couldn't reach bottom. . . . I—was always afraid to try. I guess it joins with an underground stream down there. . . ." Her voice trailed off.

Trevannon squinted into the water, aligning his gaze with a deep-shafting ray of sunlight. "A deep one, all right."

"Come on!" Her tone was sharp and querulous with the savage rein-around of her Appaloosa's head, and she kicked it into a hard trot. Repeatedly baffled by this girl's moods till he became resigned to them, Trevannon shook his head and followed.

When he'd ranged up beside her, he commented briefly, "Good way to ruin a good horse's mouth, that."

"I know," she said complacently. "What's cruelty? Just the other day, I saw Tige kick a horse in the stomach."

"Not meanly, I'll wager you didn't," Trevannon told her. "Sometimes a balky one can be cured by a kick in the belly." He had noted Tige Menefee's miraculous touch with animals that morning, and he added, "That Tige, he's half horse himself."

"He can be led like one, that's for sure," Andrea observed.

A man, Trevannon thought, gave his loyalty, his guts and soul, to her, and it meant less to her than a new toy would. And oddly, perhaps, she was neither stupid nor cruel— rather, oversensitive, in a way that had made her easily receptive to whatever warping forces had stunted her growing mind till there wasn't an honest feeling left in her. Likely her mother's doing.

Reminded of Mrs. Congreve, he said grimly, "I'll want to talk to your mother when we get back."

The big, lofty parlor of the Kaysee main house was a man's room, with its plain furniture, massive fieldstone fireplace, smoke-blackened ceiling rafters, and walls hung with bright Navajo blankets, antique rifles, crossed sabers, dueling pistols and trophy heads of grizzly, bighorn, and mule deer. Trevannon noticed Mrs. Congreve's cold and disapproving appraisal of the room as Andrea pushed her wheel chair into the parlor. Guessed that she was already planning a refurnishing that would erase the impact of Kilrain Carter's dominant personality from the house.

Mrs. Congreve adjusted a laprobe that covered her knees; her thin, arthritic fingers gripped the cane across her lap, tapping it impatiently on one chair wheel. "Well, Mr. Trevannon? You wish to tell me something?"

Trevannon was slacked in a leather-covered chair, his long legs crossed. "Yes'm." The chair creaked heavily as he leaned forward, elbows on knees and revolving his hatbrim between his hands. His ordinary courtesy to women was instinctive, but he knew there would be no mincing of words with this woman; physically helpless, she had an inner, driving ruthlessness that must be met by a tight rein.

"Mrs. Congreve," he said bluntly, "when your daughter hired me last night, she hinted that I'd be expected to keep Kaysee clear of any and all settlers."

"Andrea has already told me that you bothered reasoning with the Canaanites," she replied brittlely. "I must say, sir, that I consider this an utter waste of breath and time."

"Then," Trevannon observed flatly, "driving 'em off by force *was* your idea."

Mrs. Congreve said coolly, "Treat's, first . . . and I agreed. Hardly an original procedure; Kilrain Carter believed it was the only way to handle that trash. Evidently you believe otherwise?"

"I do. And told Ephraim Waybeck he could homestead that strip along the upper creek he wants with no interference."

The crippled woman was utterly motionless except for the slight flare of her fine nostrils. "I see. Exactly what kind of a cattleman do you consider yourself, sir?"

"An old-time one, like Carter was. But one with sense enough to know the day of open range is going . . . fast. Time's past when ranches were few enough to grab all the land they could hold. The Homestead Act ain't new, but the little people're beginning to see what it can mean for them . . . taking advantage of it. The law stands with them." He hesitated, tasting the strangeness of his next words. "I stand with the law."

She laid down her reply flatly and coldly. "You were hired principally to handle those farmers. For the reason that you seemed to be the man who could hold Kaysee intact—*for us*."

Trevannon's tone matched hers. "I'll give it to you straight, way I did to Ephraim Waybeck. I'll have all of

Kaysee's patented land properly surveyed, the boundaries marked off. I'll even hold Kaysee's open range against everyone who's got no more legal claim than us. But I'll make no move to stop the Canaanites or anyone else from proving up government homesteads on any open range. I told Waybeck he could stake out where he wants, provided he switches to cattle—no cropping this valley. If I can solve this thing without shedding blood, I mean to. That's my way. Take it or leave it."

Mrs. Congreve's ravaged face framed the thinnest smile. "Tell me why you came to me with this—not to my daughter."

"Sized you as the real power here."

"You are observant. Do you hear well, too? Because you are through here, Mr. Trevannon. Get your things and get out."

"No," Andrea said very gently. Her lips were touched by a faint, speculative smile; her dark violet gaze did not leave Trevannon.

Mrs. Congreve snapped imperiously, "What? What did you say?"

"I said no, Mother. Wes isn't fired." Andrea's smile held, and she did not even glance at her mother. "Aren't I the owner of Kaysee? With the right to hire or fire as I choose? Wes stays."

Mrs. Congreve drew a shuddering breath, let it out. "Darling," she faltered, "are you going to start behaving badly again? Mother knows what's best for us—"

"Kilrain never cared what you thought, Mother," Andrea said softly. "Here is another man who doesn't." She gave Trevannon a full and dazzling smile. "Do whatever you think is best, Wes."

Trevannon rose with a nod at Mrs. Congreve's sudden and deathly paleness. He said quietly, "Better take care of your mother." He walked softly from the room, stepping out onto the veranda. The dying sun slanted thinly against his eyes before he clamped on his hat. He hadn't realized it was this late, and now aware of belly-gnawings of hunger, he swung toward the cookshack. Wondering what had prompted Andrea's newest whim, even to defying her mother's will. . . .

He halted just within its doorway, feeling a wary shock at sight of Bill Treat seated at the foot of the table, eating with the crew. Treat's coffeecup stopped halfway to his lips and he set it down carefully, breaking the crew's sudden watching silence.

"That offer of a job still open?"

"You had your choice this morning, Treat. You made it."

Treat slowly settled his scarred hands to the table. His murky glance lifted with no surliness. He said heavily, "A man works an outfit best years of his life, raises himself to foreman. Then a younger buck whips him and throws him out on his ear. Hard thing to take. Maybe I earned that. But I earned my job too, took a lot of sweat, a lot out of me. Ain't so young I can start from scratch again, ain't so old I can't still make a top hand in this or any damn outfit you can name. Besides, man grubs and sleeps at a place that long, it gets in his bones. Wasn't easy for me to come back after this mornin'. And I won't beg from no man. But I'm askin', mister."

The silence hung again as he concluded; Trevannon's glance shuttled from one face to the next. Expressionless each, yet in each a kindred emotion reflected. Not a man of them liked Bill Treat, but it wasn't Treat as an individual that concerned them. Each man saw himself in another man whose life was his, who had sweated and frozen by his side in a grueling job, who had shared the barren dwellings of cookshack and bunkhouse that were their only homes. A man who had known his job and done it well for many years. You might overthrow such a man if you were strong enough and he deserved it, as Treat richly had, but you didn't kick him out like a dog. Treat was too proud to beg, humble enough to return, and this, too, impressed them.

Trevannon's first reaction was instant suspicion. What the hell was Treat up to? *Go slow now*, he cautioned himself;

this wasn't what he had expected of the deposed foreman, but men could change. Or adapt to changed circumstances, anyway. Old Gabe Morrow's eyes mirrored the same steady question as the others', and this decided Trevannon.

He nodded wearily, saying, "Hang up your hat, Treat," as he skirted the table to take his seat.

CHAPTER 10

KILRAIN CARTER WAS TO BE BURIED THE AFTERNOON following Treat's return to Kaysee. A mile from the ranch was an old Indian burial ground which had also served over the years for the interment of men who had died in the service of the ranch. Bill Treat knew that Carter had been anything but a sentimentalist, but long observation had told him that men worked harder and better for that of which they felt themselves an integral part; his consideration for the dead was one of various provisions by which he bound his men to loyal service.

The crew invariably got a day off for the burial; the corpse got a fine casket and a long eulogy given by the parson of Coldbrook's single community church; the parson got a generous fee. Carter would have scorned the final rites, and the words that Gabe Morrow, longest in Kaysee service, would speak would be brief and blunt; a wooden marker and the pine coffin containing the Old Man's mortal remains were fashioned by the crew in a couple of hours that morning.

The men, togged out in their somber best, followed in mounted file the jolting wagon holding the pine box. Bill Treat waited till the slow-pacing procession was a brief distance from the ranch. Then he began to cant forward in his saddle, rubbing his stomach, his face tight and wry.

Old Gabe Morrow, his toil-bent and desiccated frame looking incongruous in the neat, ancient suit he wore,

84

glanced at him. He asked, with no sympathy, "Somethin' you ate, Bill?"

"Guess so," Treat grimaced. "Gut was actin' up all morning."

For the next quarter mile he continued to grimace and grunt till Wes Trevonnon, riding up behind the wagon with Andrea Carter, fell back beside him, told him curtly, "If you're sick, get on back to the ranch."

Treat swallowed as if against nausea, gave a painful nod and swung his mount out of the column. He put his horse slowly down the backtrail till they were out of sight. Then quirted the animal savagely. . . .

He was filled with calm certainty as he turned his piebald into the corral. He knew every nook and cranny of this layout in his mind's eye. Logically, he guessed, Trevannon would have buried the bank loot. The first thing to look for was freshly turned dirt. The funeral party had been moving slowly, and he had plenty of time. He toted his saddle and bridle to the harness shed, toed open the door and went through. He slung his hull and blankets over a saddle pole, tossed his bridle over a peg, then turned to survey the dark interior of the shed. He meant to cover the inside of each dirt-floored building with special care; here a man would have time to bury an object without likelihood of discovery; the heavy shadows that filled this windowless shed made it especially choice.

Treat lifted a bull's-eye lantern from a peg, lighted it, and began a slow circuit of the walls, carefully scanning the ground by low-held lanternlight. Almost at once he found the telltale freshness in a rear corner where the clay floor had been boot-stamped and smoothed to restore its hard-packed texture. He stooped and touched it. Still moist . . . freshly dug not over a day earlier. He set the lantern down, hunted for and found a shovel hanging from a nail. Eagerly he attacked the stubborn hardpan.

Five perspiring minutes later he hit a yielding bundle. Feverishly he cleared the dirt away and hauled up the filthy grain sack. Struggled with its knotted mouth, cursing and sweating. Finally he spilled out the neat, clean packets of greenbacks in their brown half-wrappers.

He knelt in the flickering lantern glow, thumbing through the large-denomination bills: sweat broke out afresh on Treat's face. His hands trembled. Far more money than he'd ever seen at one time, even on cattle-buying trips. Temptation threaded his insides like a boring worm, but he put it aside. Kaysee was the central stake in his life, and this money would buy back the position that was his meat and drink.

He returned the money to its sack, jammed it in the pocket of his cheap suitcoat, and skirted a barn as he headed up for the main house. Best to establish an understanding with the old lady right now. She'd always quietly despised him for a thick brute, and he'd cordially hated her for it. But his hate was tempered by a certain awed respect for her cold gentility, her ruthless immorality which he'd sensed, and she was nobody's fool either. . . . Get on her good side, make her see how far they could go together, and maybe even . . . Andrea. By God, he might even stand a chance there.

He tramped onto the veranda and tapped diffidently on the door. Mrs. Congreve's brittle invitation to enter came at once. Treat halted just inside the door. She turned her wheel chair slowly from the window, her usual icy regard at his presence lessened by a distant but definite curiosity.

"Good afternoon, Mr. Treat."

"Wanted to talk to you alone, ma'am. If you can spare a minute."

"A crippled woman's time, sir, is hardly that valuable to her or to anyone else." There was an acrid bitterness to her tone that alerted Treat. Trouble between her and Andrea? Maybe. "You seem," she went on, "to have wanted this talk badly enough to desert the funeral cortege. Please sit down."

Treat settled his bulk on a leather chair facing her, his hat dangling between his fingers, certain now that there were cross-currents he'd missed. He'd half expected a sharp rebuff at first; instead she was almost cordial. Confidently he told what he'd learned from Sheriff Vandermeer, that all signs pointed to Wes Trevannon as the bank robber. That he'd agreed to search Kaysee for the stolen money. He dipped into his bulging pocket and lifted out the grain sack.

"You—found the money then?"

Treat hefted the sack lightly in a thick palm. "Twenty thousand dollars, ma'am."

Only Mrs. Congreve's eyes betrayed her sharp exultance. "Ah-h," she breathed. "That puts you in a bargaining position, Mr. Treat."

Treat frowned. "I figured—"

"That I would be unhappy at this intelligence? On the contrary. It's true that I first endorsed discharging you . . . giving Mr. Trevannon your place. That was before he decided to handle the Canaanites with a light hand. He proposes to let them take up their former homesteads, provided that they raise cattle." Mrs. Congreve's fingers taloned whitely around the arms of her chair; she leaned forward in her intensity. "You know what this will mean; our open range is the richest in the valley. The breakthrough of a few successful homesteaders will bring in a flood. I did not—" She hesitated. "I will not mince words; I believe that you and I understand each other. I did not manipulate my daughter's marriage into Kaysee so that I could fritter out my days as a confined, unwanted invalid. But Kilrain Carter was a hard man; he wielded the only whip on Kaysee. His death gave me a reason for hope.

"I had thought I could control Andrea, and, through her, Trevannon . . . whom I will not deny I thought a better man than you. But she is becoming soft on that drifter; my hold on her is weakening. I fired him, and she countermanded it—to my face." Her voice softened to a faint hiss. "Kaysee without its open range is nothing. I, without a whiphand here, am nothing. *Now* do you understand why I will not grieve if this Trevannon is removed?"

Treat stared. *By God, she's a hungry one!* Power-hungry . . . He'd sensed it before, but hadn't realized the intensity of her need. "Yes, ma'am," he said softly, "I surely do . . . and how do we stand?"

Mrs. Congreve leaned back, her eyes half-closed. "I think I can safely promise—you'll have your old job back . . . once I have back my daughter. Removing Trevannon's influence will insure that."

Treat gently cuffed the grain sack against his hat and said nothing.

Her eyes widened sharply. "That's what you want, isn't it?"

"Yes'm, partly."

"Partly? Oh-h." Her fragile lips formed a faint, ironic smile that made Treat stir uneasily. "You haven't relinquished your designs on my daughter, eh? I see. How very primitive. Might those designs include, perhaps— marriage?"

Treat swallowed hard, disciplined his single-minded lust, plunged with a muttered, "Yes'm. If she'll have me."

Mrs. Congreve's soft laugh was paper-dry. "You mean, if *I'll* have you."

"Ma'am," Treat said, anger carrying him to boldness, "this ranch is my life. I'd die before seein' it tore to pieces by a pack of cropper dogs. Reckon you know that. Kaysee'll need a man like that at the reins. Long's your daughter holds the only authority here, how can you be sure she won't overrule me? As her husband, I could damn well assure you there'd be no soft-pedalin' on any sodders!"

"I have no doubt of it," Mrs. Congreve said evenly. "I have no doubt either that if you had a legal hold on Kaysee, my own position would be relegated to precisely that which I held when Kilrain Carter was alive—a helpless nonentity. Also, whatever you may have thought, I am not without gentler feelings. My daughter means a great deal to me— and I will not see her bedded in a sty."

Treat's fists knotted in black, bitter fury; he set his jaw to control its tremor. "Think that over, lady. Just now I'm a pig you happen to need."

"Quite so. But I believe your vaunted love for Kaysee is enough to hold you."

"Listen, I can get up now and walk out that—"

"Can you, Mr. Treat? Can you really?"

For a moment they locked stares till Treat's fell sullenly from that bright, mocking contempt. *The old bitch has me by the heels and she knows it,* he raged silently. With an effort he achieved self-control, said very softly, "There'd be nothing that'd change your mind?"

"Money," she said at once and flatly.

Treat blinked.

"Money," she repeated gently. "For two reasons. First—a man can change, even you. I'm not deceived about blue blood and gentle breeding, that sort of rot. I come from one of Boston's oldest families, the Godwins. Do you know how my ancestors came by their wealth? The original Godwin was a London guttersnipe who rose as a pirate freebooter, raiding Spanish merchantmen, pillaging and murdering. His sons became New England merchants who augmented their ill-gotten inheritance as crooked and cut-throat pirates of the business world. You see, money does work wonders, even on swine. Even you, Mr. Treat, could become bathed, broadclothed, mannered, and perfectly respectable . . . in time, for stupidity is not one of your undesirable characteristics. A man like that could win my daughter—with my help."

"Two reasons for money, you said," Treat declared harshly.

"Just so. The next man to marry Andrea will have to pay her mother a very sizable dowry. I do not share your great love of Kaysee ranch, Mr. Treat, nor of your raw, brawling West. I would much prefer power on my own terms, in my own society. That society is Beacon Hill of Boston, the circle of snobs who disowned me when I married a weak, ne'er-do-well, Curt Congreve. I would like to return there with the means to buy back—position. And the pleasure of watching certain people crawl for me. It really is amazing what a universal language money speaks."

Treat licked his dry lips. The deadly and disillusioned cynicism of this woman made a man's spine crawl. "Sort of lets me out," he muttered gloomily.

Mrs. Congreve's pale lips formed her thin, wicked smile. "Cheer up, Mr. Treat. You will have your old sty back, after all. . . ."

It was well toward evening before the funeral party had returned to the ranch that afternoon. The crew off-saddled and straggled toward the bunkhouse, talking in hushed voices. Trevannon, as he unsaddled the sorrel, reflected soberly that it was as though a giant pine had crashed to earth, leaving an empty space against the sky. He remembered the stories of Kilrain Carter, a legendary giant, he'd heard over the years, and today he had helped lay that legend to rest.

He was conscious of Andrea Carter standing at his elbow, impatiently tapping a horsehair quirt against her palm. She wore a black riding habit and hat with a dark veil . . . fashionable widows' weeds that set off her slender fullness. Part of the travesty of her mourning, Trevannon thought wearily as he turned to her horse and uncinched the sidesaddle. He began to swing it off, only to find it held in an iron grasp, and he looked across the saddle swell into the murky hatred of Tige Menefee's eyes. With a sigh he let go of the saddle, and Tige took it and stalked silently from the corral. Wes picked up his own saddle and swung to face Andrea.

Her eyes glowed innocently through the veil. "Tige always takes care of my riding gear. He's very jealous about that, you know. But he's a dear, really. . . . I was thinking that you must be tired of cookshack grub. Why don't you have supper with Mother and me?"

"That an order?" he asked unsmilingly.

She did smile, quite archly. "I can make it one."

He shook his head. "Better not."

"Why, that sounds like an ultimatum."

"You could say that."

Andrea kept smiling, tilting her head a little to regard him. "Nobody tells you your way, do they?" she murmured. "That's what I like most about you."

There was a deep softening in her face that made Wes uneasy. He had believed that her flying in the face of her mother's will by refusing to fire him had been a typical whim; now he wasn't so sure. She had openly flirted with him before the crew, which had accounted for the sullen, subdued air that hung over the whole proceeding. The simple ethics of these men were his own, running counter to the whole behavior of this capricious, moody girl. True, they'd all made a joke of the patent farce of the Old Man marrying a woman little more than a third his age, but in their eyes, aberrant behavior in a "respectable" woman was shocking. . . .

But Trevannon's concern went deeper. Not missing the wealth of hidden meaning behind her light words and looks, he was left perplexed and worried. In a way he liked this girl for all her unpredictable moods; he wanted to help her, but hadn't anticipated that she might want something of him he couldn't give. He couldn't deny the strange attraction of her childlike innocence and womanly beauty; it had possessed other men, could engulf him too unless he kept on his guard. . . .

"I'll be going," he growled and walked off, with the silver trill of her laughter following. He left his saddle at the harness shed and tramped to the bunkhouse, met Gabe Morrow halfway there.

"Treat ain't in the bunkhouse," the old puncher told him. "Thought at first he might've strayed off the trail on his way back, sick as he was—"

"He made it back—that piebald horse of his is in the corral."

"Thought of that." Gabe paused worriedly. "Sick man should be in his bunk. Where'n hell—?"

"You look around the cookshack, corrals, stables. I'll try the house. You find him, sing out."

Gabe nodded and headed goutily for a haybarn. Wes

headed toward the main house and its outbuildings, set off from the working part of the ranch. He started with the big carriage shed which faced away from the house. Stepped through its big double doors and halted there to accustom his eyes to the musty gloom.

A boot whispered against the clay floor.

"Treat?"

Moving toward Trevannon, the bull-shouldered hulk of the ex-foreman took sudden shape in the half-darkness. The uptilted gun in his fist glinted against the late-westering daylight. There was something bulky in his other hand.

"What is—"

"Shut up," Treat rasped. He took two more steps to squarely front the taller man. His breathing was a harsh sweep. "I've been waitin' for this. . . . You looking for something, maybe?" He lifted the bulky object from his side. "Like this?"

As Trevannon's eyes flicked down, widened on the grain sack, Treat struck, savagely and without warning. His gun barrel slashed along Trevannon's temple, staggering him. He hit again, driving the drifter to his hands and knees.

Through a swimming blur Trevannon saw Treat's legs and tried to grab them. Treat stepped back and drove a boot into his side. He tried to flinch away from the knife-like pain, gagging. A second kick snapped his chin back, drove him sprawling on his side. He saw Treat loom above, saw the shining arc the gun made coming down again, and helplessly awaited it. He felt it explode against the top of his skull; his dizzy senses pinwheeled off into blackness.

CHAPTER 11

Consciousness reached for his mind like a gray and flickering pulse before it riptided fully back in shattering pain. Dried blood crusted his eyelids; he forced them open.

Tied across the saddle with his legs on one side, his head and arms swinging on the other, his body rocked limply to his horse's gait. He saw the rutted dust of a road moving beneath, and nausea boiled into his throat and he retched into the dust. Gasping, painfully he turned his head to see Bill Treat's bulky silhouette riding ahead, a lead rope in his fist fastened to the bridle of Trevannon's own bay gelding. Treat, looking back over his shoulder, gave a dry chuckle.

Trevannon squirmed and fought the ropes till his body began to slip free; Treat, with a curse, halted and swung down. Unfastened the ropes and gave a yank on Trevannon's belt that dumped him to the ground.

"I make it you're feisty enough to sit a saddle," he oberved.

Wes shut his eyes against the throbbing fire in his skull, lay motionless awhile till sense and feeling flowed back.

Treat rooted him viciously in the side with a boot. "Come on, get up there!"

With an effort he pulled himself to a sitting position, caught a stirrup and hauled his body upright. He leaned a panting moment against the bay's flank, toed into stirrup and heaved himself astride, leaning his face sickly against its neck.

Treat unfastened the lead rope and handed up his bridle. "You ride ahead." Treat's palm slashed across the bay's rump, started it moving. He mounted his piebald and fell in behind.

For a full five minutes, Trevannon let the bay pick its way without guidance, his face bowed into the mane. He set his teeth then and half-lifted his head. The landscape dizzily swam, settled to firm outlines.

Sunset's final flush was dying against the black-toothed rim of horizon. It was not quite full twilight, but the sunglare had softened bright hues to old-rose and gray. His eyes hurt, and he was grateful for the muted light and the coming coolness. He place landmarks and judged that they were several miles west of the ranch. He had never been to the valley settlement of Coldbrook, but had no doubt that was their destination; the wagon road beneath was well-marked by ranch traffic. He glanced at the dipping sun and decided he had been unconscious for over an hour. Andrea Carter had mentioned that Coldbrook was ten miles from Kaysee. They might have covered half the distance by this time. . . .

Without turning he spoke, shocked at the broken croak his voice made: "You got a warrant, Treat?"

"Citizen's arrest," Treat answered amusedly. "Man who steals twenty thousand dollars makes himself free game in an open field."

"So you talked to the sheriff, put two and two together. I had you all wrong."

"Outsmarted you, eh? Never occur to you why I really came back?"

"That," Wes said softly, now looking back. "Also I figured you'd crowd your chance harder . . . like putting a bullet in me, claiming self-defense."

"Man," Treat laughed, "you bought yourself free room and board on the territory—maybe twenty years of it— when you took that money. Now why should I spoil that?"

Trevannon nodded weakly, dropped his head back to the horse's mane as though he'd given it all up.

Actually his mind was racing desperately over his situation, assessing it. That backward glance had shown him Treat comfortably slack in his saddle, his gun in holster. Contemptuously careless, and not without cause. Even should his prisoner try a break, he could easily put a bullet in his back; the country was flat and open, only thinly stippled with blocks of timber. Without moving his bowed head, Trevannon's questing gaze took in a dense stand of young trees whose lower aisles were crowded with heavy brush . . . just ahead, the road cutting through its center.

It was a long chance, but it might be his last one. He could never have pulled it off in full daylight; the thickening twilight gave him a bare edge. And Treat had read him aright: a man for whom freedom was the breath of life would die a thousand lingering deaths behind prison walls. Better to take the slender gamble, he thought bleakly. If it went wrong, he'd still lose less in the long run.

They reached the timber and rode between its dark flanks. The air was breathless and still except for the hushed *clop* of shod hoofs in the soft road dust. Without stirring his body, Trevannon flexed his sweating hands before him, tightly gripped his bridle. Smoothly coordinated the sideward wrench on his horse's head with the jab of spurs. Launched the bay hard and sideways into the brush. Crashed solidly through it and broke at once into an open glade, not halting.

Treat's shrilled curse had come even as he left the road, but he was already inside dim cover when the first shot came. It whipped foliage somewhere at his back. Trevannon spurred across the glade, saw another thicket loom darkly to his right and threw himself from the saddle into its springy top branches even as he heard Treat's crashing advance into the brush behind. His balled body plunged through the bare lower boughs and he made himself small amidst their tangle as his horse bolted on into the trees beyond.

At once Treat hauled up his mount in the little glade not three yards from where Trevannon crouched. He hoped achingly that Treat would judge his position by where his horse had stopped. Treat slowly dismounted, stood for a moment listening. Wes heard his heavy breathing, saw his body tense-postured, the steely twinkle of his drawn gun through the screening leaves.

Slowly Treat tramped forward—moving past the thicket not a yard distant, but swallowed almost at once by the close-set tree boles. With infinite care Trevannon broke off a limber branch and noiselessly detached himself from the thicket, took several long strides to reach Treat's horse. He quartered it around to face the road and slashed the switch across its rump.

The piebald squealed and plunged away toward the road. Trevannon faded back into the trees, listening to the fast-diminishing tattoo of hoofbeats as Treat, squalling curses, crashed back through the wood toward the road. He'd guess that the fugitive's ruse had involved taking his horse, which was what Trevannon wanted him to think—giving Wes a chance to reach his bay, with Treat left afoot halfway between town and the ranch. The piebald probably wouldn't stop till he reached his home corral, and the time it took Treat to get back and fork a fresh horse would give Trevannon a wide lead.

Quickly he groped through the timber till he found the bay standing quietly almost at its far end. Once in leather, he nudged through the remaining grove and hit up an easy lope. . . .

Now, he knew bitterly, there was no choice left him. Treat's uncovering of the money would pin the identity of the bank robber squarely on him, the only stranger at Kaysee. That was the price he'd paid for underestimating the squat foreman. He must keep riding, clear of the valley, far out of the territory, before he could draw another safe breath. Something else he hadn't expected was that this knowledge really hurt. A man had to exonerate himself in his own eyes, and he'd made a good start here. Now he must drop everything and run, and every fiber of his being rebelled against the fact.

He thought of the Canaanites . . . and mostly of Calla Waybeck. That made it harder, for she had stayed in his mind after their brief talk. He wanted to see her again before he went on . . . *But what then?* he wondered bleakly. *What good would it do, for you or her?* He considered that more thoughtfully. Just maybe he could do her and the others one bit of good. There was still Cassius McQuayle, the man he hadn't met, whose name had cropped up repeatedly and who might be using the Canaanites for a hidden purpose, something that might hurt Kaysee too.

If he could offer Ephraim Waybeck proof of the perfidy of a man he trusted, put him on guard, he could still bring some good out of his own brief part in this affair. Too, partly at least, it was a kind of last gesture, like a damnfool kid showing off for his girl. He wanted very much not to leave Calla Waybeck thinking ill of him, as she must if he simply vanished without explanation.

Meantime the broad head start he had on Treat would give him time. He didn't know Cassius McQuayle; the man might be an iron ramrod or a fragile reed, easily broken. *You can find out fast enough,* Trevannon though grimly. . . . Without hesitation he swung his horse back toward the wagon road.

It was full dark when the black-blocked buildings of town grew into view. Trevannon rode down Coldbrook's single avenue, through the long rectangles of saffron glow out-thrown by street windows. He spotted the general trade store and tied his horse at the rail and went in.

The proprietor was about to close up, but his first resentment faded at the sizable order of grub staples Trevannon gave him against the trail ahead, when he expected to hole up and sleep by day, travel by night and avoid towns till he was out of the territory. The storekeeper was brisk and officious; it didn't take him long to assemble Trevannon's wants, dump them in a flour sack. As Trevannon paid, he asked casually where Lawyer McQuayle lived.

"In his hotel room where he's always lived," the proprietor snapped. "Always works late in his office, though. Want to see him now, suggest you try there; professional building across the street."

Trevannon thanked him and left, lingering at the tie rail to tie the sack of supplies to his saddle horn. Then he cut across to the professional building where he saw a single light burning in a second-story window.

Wes paused at the entrance to scan the street, a mechanical precaution. His gaze narrowed down on the adobe jail across the way a block down. His mouth went dry. No mistaking the broad, towering outline of the man lounging in the doorway . . . Jans Vandermeer. Cal Kittredge had impressively described the sheriff: ". . . built like a mountain . . . man you couldn't miss." So Vandermeer's search for the robber had brought him to Coldbrook . . . Of course; it was Vandermeer who'd tipped off Bill Treat.

Just now the sheriff's head turned; he was talking over his shoulder to someone in the office. Trevannon let out a long-held breath and went lightly up the staircase, taking the steps three at a time. The second-floor corridor was dark, but he saw a fine slit of lamplight beneath a door halfway down. He catfooted to it, gently palmed the doorknob and turned it, an instant later closed the door behind him.

Sallow lamplight profiled a man sitting at a rolltop desk, hunched over it busily. A swivel chair creaked under his slight weight as he swung about. He was a frail specter of a man in his mid-sixties whose wispy white hair framed a slack-wrinkled and benign face. His blue eyes held a tired but facile kindliness, and his age-rusty black suit lent an air of honorable poverty. He tossed his pencil onto a scattering of legal-looking documents and removed his iron-rimmed spectacles with a genial smile. "Can I do—"

Cassius McQuayle dropped his statement in mid-air and let it hang unfinished. Trevannon's face reflected his mood. Sudden alarm washed across McQuayle's; he reached slowly for a desk drawer by his knee.

"Better if you didn't," Trevannon said gently.

"Wh—what?"

"Just some talk." Wes walked to the desk, slung a hip over its corner. Warily eying him, McQuayle picked up a tobacco plug by his elbow, with palsied fingers sheared off a wad with a penknife and stowed it in the pouch of his cheek. He cudded it slowly and uneasily. Trevannon ignored the nervous ritual, staring stonily into McQuayle's eyes.

"I got some question. You better have the answers."

McQuayle's benign blandness drained away, baring a cold slyness. Calla Waybeck had been right about him, Trevannon thought then. "Who are you?" MacQuayle asked in a genial tone.

"Mister, you don't ask, just answer. Why you really want that land you got the Canaanites to homestead?"

"I don't know what you—" McQuayle began, and Trevannon's big hand shot out, fisted a handful of his shirt front and dragged his frail body from the chair. He forced the lawyer to his knees, twisting the high, stiff collar cruelly against the scrawny neck. Trevannon had already sized up this shyster as nothing but an oil-tongued confidence man, and he was out of patience.

"Don't waste my time," he told McQuayle. "I haven't any to spare."

"God's sake, mister—ease off—I got a bad heart—"

"Then you got good reason not to tax it. I haven't. Remember that." Trevannon let up his grip enough for the lawyer to drag air into his bruised throat. It had been far easier than he'd expected . . . a single threat, a brief show of force, and this bland little man was reduced to a quivering bundle of fright.

McQuayle now babbled out a story whose main outlines Trevannon had half-guessed. With the Homestead Act had come a host of elaborate land swindles that took ruthless legal advantage of the honor code of an earlier West, where a man's handshake was his sworn bond. Against the new land pirates, every cattleman had learned to be on his guard. Like much large-scale chincanery, McQuayle's scheme was wholly within the law. He'd seen the uselessness of this valley for other than forage crop purposes. He also knew that the federal government had forced a treaty on some nomadic Navajos which had deprived them of a large chunk of their southern stamping grounds, including most of this valley, which Kilrain Carter had tacked onto his Kaysee ranch years ago by burning out a Navajo camp. The new treaty had made the valley public domain.

McQuayle wanted a sizable strip along Kaysee's east boundary. To get it, he'd gone to the newly arrived Canaanites, and after ingratiating himself into friendship with Ephraim Waybeck, had persuaded him that this was the tract he wanted, Ephraim half-believing that Mc-Quayle's persuasive manner was part of the Providence that had guided him here. The Canaanites were diehard farmers. Within two years at the most, they would see the futility of trying to crop this land, even with the sanction of divine guidance. Rather than starve to death, they would sell their proved-up homesteads to McQuayle for next to nothing.

McQuayle's eyes flickered slyly. "And I'd have a nice piece of grass to speculate with. . . ."

"You're a liar," Trevannon said flatly. "Why that particular piece? I make it you got a get-rich-quick joker up your sleeve. Your kind never cares about slow returns, and you're an old man, too old to wait. There's something else about that land. . . ."

He reached for MacQuayle's throat again; the lawyer made a thin, bleating sound, flinched away.

"For God's sake, don't hurt me! I'll tell you!" He rubbed a shaking hand over his sagging, putty-tinged face. "I know quite a bit—about mining and mines. Used to hang around 'em a lot—"

"Selling useless stock in 'em?"

McQuayle paused uneasily. "Anyway, I was riding over that way a year ago, found gold in the beds of some creek branches on that tract. Enough to make me interested."

Trevannon said grimly, "A lot of streambeds are filled with heavy color. Don't mean a damn thing. When I was a kid, I wasted a year panning streams. Took most of my pay in an aching back."

"I spotted some auriferous outcrops," McQuayle sighed. "Like they say, gold's where you find it. Auriferous rock, though, can mean rich deposits. I spent several days digging shallow test pits . . . and carefully covering them up again. Time and again, I hit solid veins, pockets of the stuff." He paused; his face in the lamplight had a sick, yellowish cast. "That whole boundary strip is filthy with the stuff . . . placer deposits. A man who owned the land could set up mining equipment, large-scale operations. Chance of a lifetime. . . ." His voice trailed; his chin dropped to his chest.

Trevannon took him by the shoulder, gave a hard shake. "Anyone plowin' that land'd be sure to run into some gold pockets."

"Know that," McQuayle said wearily. "That's why the Canaanites were ideal for my purpose. They believe wealth, the wordly pleasures it buys, is the worst curse under the sun. Unlike most people, they don't turn their backs on their beliefs when it's convenient. And they wouldn't let word of the gold get out, knowing that everybody in the country would swarm in to stake a claim if they did."

"And you think they'd ever sell out to you, when they found out what you was after?"

Cassius McQuayle smiled feebly. "It was admittedly a gamble—but I think it would go something like this: I know Ephraim Waybeck well. He's no fool in his way, but that childlike faith of his will always betray him. He reads the real good in people like a printed page—his big weakness is, he also reads good into people when there is none, simply because he wants to believe it. Then too—while I have no illusions about myself, I can create a most convincing illusion of myself for all except folk with a streak of—shall we say, honest cynicism—like yourself. And like old Ephraim's daughter-in-law Calla, a perceptive young woman who does not think in the same terms as her compatriots. She plainly distrusts me. Fortunately, a woman's opinions carry small weight. . . .

"Now—I would go to Ephraim Waybeck wearing a contrite face, with many apologies for recommending this property that turned out so badly for them. And offer to make amends by buying it up. Despite the bad state of my finances, I would feel I must make what small atonement I can afford. Ephraim would be most touched—and gladly sell me the land with its riches which are useless to him, but which in my benevolent hands would be used judiciously and wisely as a force for good."

Trevannon was silent, regarding the old con man with a kind of reluctant admiration for a born scoundrel's elaborate foresight. "That's long-range guessing," he said.

"I told you it was a gamble," McQuayle whispered. "God knows I've no physical courage. But a confidence man without confidence—what's that? These were the stakes which would climax—and justify—these many years of petty schemes, mostly failures. I was casting all my experience and a few thousand dollars I'd saved into one magnificent pot." He glanced up with a faint, sly hope. "I wonder—how many people will believe this story?"

"Calla Waybeck," Trevannon said promptly. "And likely Ephraim, if it comes from me. I met him; he sort of took a fancy to me. He won't be particularly happy, either, about you stampedin' his crazy brother-in-law into cutting Kilrain Carter in half with a shotgun. . . ."

McQuayle's eyes jerked wildly. "Who said I did?"

"One or two people who figure Bodie Teece was no

killer, for all his ranting. They figure somebody put a bug in his ear—something Teece said before he shot Carter points that way. They think you're a likely candidate. After meetin' you, so do I. You're the kind could talk a rattler out of his fangs.''

"Now I ask you . . . do I look like a man who'd plan a murder?"

"Not directly, no. But if the stakes was high enough, and you could push it along with no danger to yourself. . . . why not? This way you couldn't be touched, no matter what anybody suspected.''

McQuayle was too defeated to argue. "Ah-h . . . what's the difference? Bodie hated the Devil even above Kilrain Carter. I told him Carter was known to hold Black Masses . . . that he was gathering the forces of darkness to crush the Canaanites. Old fool was ready to believe anything bad about Carter. I didn't think he'd bother to mention to anyone where he picked up the notion.'' His eyes narrowed. "That might have turned the trick—or possibly something else did. You see, you can't prove a thing one way or the other. Now, damn you,'' with a sudden flare of spirit, "will you get off my back?"

McQuayle settled himself in his chair, with movements like those of a very old and tired man. "I had the idea, anyway,'' he murmured. "The glorious taste of it. The one thing you can't take away.''

Suddenly this little man and his office were very shabby and unimpressive, and Trevannon, scowling down at him, could find no words small enough to waste on him. He stood and walked quietly to the door. All he could do now was tell Andrea Carter and Ephraim Waybeck what he had learned. It would not solve all their troubles, he knew bleakly; those were only beginning, but cutting the ground from under McQuayle would end a lot of grief before it got started. In any case, he couldn't do more. . . .

He palmed open the door and stepped into the murky hallway. Instantly froze as the bobbing flare of a lantern appeared in the stairwell, filling the corridor with its diffused glare. Trevannon's hand brushed his holster, reaching for the gun Treat had taken, before he remembered. He stopped dead, facing the stone-faced giant coming up the stairs with a lantern in one hamlike fist, a leveled gun in the other. Jans Vandermeer had caught up at last. And crowding behind the sheriff's bulk was the grinning face of Bill Treat.

CHAPTER 12

SHERIFF VANDERMEER'S STOLID GRIMNESS HARDLY RELAXED with the taking of Wes Travannon and the recovery of the twenty thousand in bank loot which Bill Treat has turned over to him. It was all in the day's work; his ready smile never touched the other lines of his craggy face. When he'd gotten Cassius McQuayle's assurance that he was unhurt, though badly shaken, he glanced at the small heavy safe in one corner of McQuayle's dingy office and said that tomorrow he'd start back for Cedar Wells with his prisoner; Lawyer McQuayle's safe looked to be a sturdy one, and might he leave the twenty thousand dollars there overnight?

McQuayle apathetically agreed, and the sheriff watched him dial open his safe, place the grain sack of money inside, and close it. The sheriff then thanked Bill Treat for his help, said a stolid goodnight, and left with his prisoner, headed for the jail.

Bill Treat lingered in McQuayle's office, slacking into the visitor's chair, feeling elatedly expansive as he fired up a cheap cigar. Enjoying McQuayle's trembling reaction as the shyster sat hunched in his swivel chair. "Put a scare into you, did he, old man?" Treat asked with mock sympathy.

McQuayle stirred a hand feebly, only now glancing at Treat. "I don't understand how you—the sheriff—happened to come here."

Treat was feeling ebullient and boastful. He told how he'd arranged with the sheriff to capture Trevannon, whom they'd deduced was the Cedar Wells bank robber. When he'd turned up the necessary evidence—the bank loot—he was to bring Trevannon in for arrest. On the way Trevannon had escaped and set him afoot, hoorawing off his horse.

"What he didn't know, I raised that piebald from a colt," Treat concluded, chuckling. "He don't go far from old Bill even when he's stampeded. . . . I whistled him up and hustled on to Coldbrook. Figured Trevannon might cut for here first to pick up some grub. Sure enough, found his horse hitched in front of the general store, sack of grub tied on. Old Murfree was just closin' up. I give him Trevannon's description. Said he'd asked about Cassius McQuayle. Well, your window was still lighted—that cinched it. So I fetched Dutchy Vandermeer on the double." He leaned forward curiously, lacing his thick fingers together. "What did he want with you anyhow?"

"None of your business."

Treat's gaze narrowed. "Wouldn't have to do with the Canaanites, would it?"

A sudden wariness flickered in McQuayle's faded eyes before he covered it.

Treat laughed. "Hell, man, you can play Father Christmas to them simple-minded sodders; a man who's been around can see through you like glass. That bastard Trevannon's no fool, neither am I. Don't know what your game is, 'cept that eggin' plowmen onto a couple sections of graze that wa'n't made for plowin' don't make sense on the face of it. . . ."

McQuayle shaped a strange, hopeless smile. "What's the difference now? Trevannon knows anyway. About the gold."

"Gold!" It left Treat in an explosive grunt. He came out of his chair and took three long strides to McQuayle's side, set his fists on his hips and glowered down at the smaller man. "Cass, you got some medicine to make. And it better be straight talk."

A part of Treat's mind hung avidly on McQuayle's

droned, dull-spoken explanation, while his thoughts leaped ahead with a mounting exultation. . . .

Till a few hours ago, when he had reached a dissatisfying agreement with Mrs. Congreve, two passions had centered Bill Treat's life. Driving passions, yet limited both, for he wasn't by nature a complex man. One was Kaysee, the other was Kilrain Carter's beautiful widow. Previously he had been satisfied with foremanship of the great ranch he'd help make; a savage lust had filled out his desire for Andrea.

Whether she'd so intended or not, Mrs. Congreve had caused Treat's ambitions to vault sky-high. The possibilities she had suggested—marriage to Andrea, coming into full control of Kaysee—had left him breathless with the sight of shining new vistas, even while he realized the hopelessness of these goals. Money was the huge drawback, the root of his frustrations. With money, he'd have Mrs. Congreve's cooperation—and then Kaysee and Andrea—and finally Mrs. Congreve herself sent back East and out of his hair for good.

He was puffing his cigar with wild excitement now . . . *gold on Kaysee!* Treat's emotional demands were simple, but his sly mind was handy at mulling over ideas, if they weren't too abstract. It busied itself at once. Rather, there was gold on public domain, a fortune waiting in the earth, unstaked and unclaimed. Even unknown, as yet, save to Cass McQuayle and now himself. *And Trevannon,* he thought viciously. . . .

McQuayle had good reason to be upset. There would be a mighty claim-rush on that land if word got out. And Trevannon, now prison-bound, had no reason to keep quiet, had good reason to reveal the lawyer's scheme to use his friends the Canaanites.

If Trevannon were somehow silenced, the scheme could go ahead as McQuayle had planned. Around this simple fact revolved the key to the wealth Treat desperately needed. Except that, instead of keeping the Canaanites off that land as he'd vowed to Mrs. Congreve, he'd be committed to insuring their successful settlement . . . at least till their homesteads were proved up and they could sell out to McQuayle.

Somehow he must trick that shrew of a Congreve woman. There were ways. If he couldn't keep her in ignorance, he'd explain that he judged Trevannon to be right on one point: that land wasn't fit for farming; the land itself would defeat them, and they'd abandon it, their failure a warning to all future sodbusters. It would be more effective than throwing them off. Yet if they took Trevannon's advice and raised cattle instead, he'd have to wait till they'd proved up their homesteads before driving them off. That could make him a lot of trouble. By God, it was all chancy enough, and no mistake. But he'd cross his bridges when they came up; the important thing was, this was his main chance and he had to grab it.

His hand dropped to McQuayle's frail shoulder, shaking it roughly. "Listen, Cass," he said with a wintry grin. "How bad you want that land? Enough to split whatever you get from it down the middle?"

McQuayle was staring vacuously at the papers on his desk, kneading his lower lip between thumb and forefinger. He glanced up wearily. "What's the difference now?"

Treat's hand tightened. "Do you?"

McQuayle winced. "Yes, damn you, I'd settle for half! But what—"

"You remember," Treat pressed, "what Trevannon said a few minutes ago when the sheriff asked him if he had anything to say?"

The lawyer frowned. "He said, 'Nothing you'd listen to.' I surmise that he's smart enough not to say anything till he gets his day in court. Then," McQuayle added bitterly, "he'll tear my idea wide open by springing it dramatically in public. . . . What's on your mind, Treat?"

"Something," Treat murmured, "that a shaky, rabbity old gent like you couldn't pull off by his lonesome. All right—Trevannon ain't about to talk. Gives us time. Not that we need a hell of a lot. Just a few hours, till the town's asleep. And then, old man, for the cost of a bullet you and I'll have our fingers in a fortune . . . not a bad trade, eh?"

The Coldbrook jail was a small stone building with the deputy's office constituting its front half; a door opened into the cell block behind where a short corridor, illumined by a lamp in a wall bracket, divided two large cells. In one, a drunk was snoring it off. Wes Trevannon stepped into the other, and Deputy Bell clanged the door shut and turned the key. Trevannon slacked onto the narrow wooden cot, crossed his legs and pillowed his folded arms behind his head.

Sheriff Vandermeer stepped close to the bars, frowning in at him. "Mr. Trevannon," he said deliberately, "I confess that you have me buffaloed. With twenty thousand stolen dollars it makes sense that you would ride far from this country with all possible haste. It does not make sense that a fleeing criminal would risk his life to save another, as you did for Mrs. Carter—but granted that he might, why should he then remain for any purpose? You are a very rash and foolish man, Mr. Trevannon, or a very complicated and clever one . . . perhaps something of both. This I don't know. Wish you now would explain yourself."

Trevannon shook his head very slightly.

Job Bell tossed the key ring up and down in his hand, glaring through the bars. "You want my opinion, he used a saddle tramp's gall to run a sandy on Mrs. Carter, then finagled himself into that foreman's job. Figured if nobody found the money, they couldn't do anything. That's simple enough."

Vandermeer shook his massive head reprovingly. "You tend to oversimplify always, Job. This is not a good thing in a man of law. It makes you overlook what else there may be under your very nose. But it is so with young men. See now: a man afraid of the law, smart or stupid, his first instinct is to run far away; he does not reason so closely as all that. No, there is something to this man that remains unsaid. Why does he visit Lawyer McQuayle? McQuayle says he comes in and demands money. For the getaway? Perhaps. But why pick on a poor attorney? Why did he not rob this thriving store where grub he buys?"

Trevannon smiled faintly, looked away from them and tilted his hat over his eyes.

Vandermeer snorted gently. "Get your sleep then. We start for Cedar Wells early tomorrow."

When the door to the office closed behind the two lawmen, Trevannon swung at once to his feet. Stoically he did not curse his bad luck, wasting time in futile regrets. You couldn't plan life; when a situation soured, you had to make the best of it. He felt the solidly mortared stones of the walls, stood on his cot to test the bars of the single high window, and calmly accepted the impregnable sturdiness of his prison. He sat on the bunk and without haste or panic pondered the problem. Only wit could help him now . . . and Vandermeer would know every jail breaker's dodge in the book. On the other hand, and as the sheriff himself had hinted, young Job's mule-set way narrowed his thinking; in a prosaic situation he'd be cautious enough, but caught off-guard by an unfamiliar one, he'd more likely act on confused impulse.

Trevannon thoughtfully studied a knothole punched through one of the two-by-eight ceiling joists overhead. Then cocked his head, listening to the drift of voices beyond the door.

". . . should get some sleep at my pa's house if you want an early start," Bell was saying. "If you think best, I'll stay the night here—he's a slippery customer."

"That would be best," Vandermeer assented, hesitating then as if for a special word of caution. Which, since he'd already criticized Bell, he didn't voice, only saying quietly, "Watch sharp, Job."

The outer office door closed behind the sheriff. Trevannon heard Bell's swivel chair creak with his settled weight. . . . Then he set quietly to work. He'd picked up not a few useful tricks during his law-dodging interlude. One was the handleless blade of a straight-edged razor, hidden in a deep slit of one of his run-down half boots. Filed very thin and lying flat within the thick, stiff leather, it had escaped even Vandermeer's practiced search of his clothing. It took five minutes to work it free of the boot. Then he took the single coarse blanket from his cot and cut three lengthwise strips from it. Working quickly, he braided the blanket strands into a tough, crude rope. He stood on his cot and stretched his height on tiptoe, straining his arms upward to poke an end of his rope through the beam knothole. He anchored it with a tight knot and then swung his full weight off the cot to test it.

The improvised length held. Trevannon climbed back to the cot and stripped off his denim jacket, bound the free end of the rope around his torso and beneath his arms, straining to take up all the slack possible. He pulled his jacket on again, buttoned it to his throat and turned up the collar. He hinged his knees and let his inert weight swing off the cot and hang suspended, slowly turning, in the center of the cell. Extended his legs and found with satisfaction that his toes swung clear of the floor. The rope ran down the back of his neck, hidden by the jacket; the razor lay concealed in his right hand, flat against the palm.

Now you look like gallows' fruit, you better act the part, ran his wry thought. He raised his voice in a strangled yell, wildly churning his arms and legs. At once Job Bell flung open the door and lunged into the corridor, halted with his jaw falling slack. "Godalmighty," he breathed, and frantically snatched the key ring from his belt.

As Bell lunged through the door, Trevannon's leg kicked back as if by painful reflex. Then he drove it savagely forward into the pit of the deputy's stomach. Bell simply melted to the floor. Crumpled there in doubled-up agony, he gagged soundlessly. Trevannon reached above his head and slashed the rope with a stroke of his razor, dropped to the floor.

He bent over Bell and jerked his gun from its holster. Said between his teeth, "Sorry, boy, you learn the hard way," as he brought the barrel down in a stiff, chopping arc behind Bell's ear. The young deputy's muscles strung hard, then he went quickly limp.

Trevannon removed Bell's gunbelt, caught him beneath the arms and hoisted him onto the bunk. Stretched him with his face to the wall and spread the blanket over him. His hard blow had been carefully placed; it would lay a man out cold for an hour or so and leave him with no worse than a bad headache and some painfully acquired wisdom.

Wes buckled on Bell's gun, locked the door behind him, glanced at the man in the other cell who snored soddenly on, and then went out to the office. He tossed the keys on Bell's desk and stepped to the door, opened it a crack to scan the street. The hitch-rack by the general store was empty; Vandermeer must have taken his horse to the livery. A tinny piano was banging away in a saloon, and a couple of men came out arm in arm, drunkenly weaving and bawling tunelessly,

> "We cleared up all the Indians,
> Drank all the alkali,
> And it's whack the cattle on, boys—
> Root hog or die. . . ."

Trevannon tugged his hatbrim low and went out, closing the door. He headed unhurried down the sidewalk, skirting the two drunks, and turned in at the livery stable. A lantern hung over a spike driven into a stall post burned dimly. No sign of the hostler . . . catching a drink, likely.

Trevannon quickly located his bay in an end stall and saddled up. But he rode out from town as though he had all the time in the world, drawling, "Howdy," to the casual greeting of an incoming rider he passed.

Beyond the last building, he lined onto the wagon road toward Kaysee, his bitter impatience set like a hot coal in his belly.

CHAPTER 13

Against that impatience, Trevannon held his horse in to conserve its strength, and it was two hours before he came in sight of ranch headquarters. From the road he could see the bunkhouse and main house were darkened, but wary of being picked up by the ranch dog he tethered his horse a good fifty yards from the buildings and hiked in, circling wide to come up on the house from the nearby grove. He'd been unconscious when Treat had taken him away; he had to assume for safety's sake that the other Kaysee people knew by now that he was a wanted fugitive. His two days' foremanship here had hardly been enough to command the crew's loyalty—of them, he'd gotten close only to Gabe Morrow. He couldn't get to Gabe without arousing the others. That left Andrea, and he wasn't sure which room was hers, knowing only that the bedroom windows opened on this side of the house.

But emerging from the grove and trotting across the yard, he found himself in luck. Lamplight filled a rectangle of a window, beyond which he glimpsed Andrea's bright crown of auburn hair. He ran silently to the window and tapped on a pane.

She was sitting on her bed, wearing a red quilted wrapper, head tilted as she brushed out her hair; it crumpled softly across the shirred collar of her robe, a darkly burnished mass shot with red-gold highlights. She quickly turned her head, lowered the hand that held her silver-chased brush. Wide-eyed, she rose and came quickly to the window, wrestled the lower sash up a couple of inches. Trevannon got his fingers beneath and shoved it higher.

Andrea went down on her knees, her fingers grasping the sill. "What happened?" she said.

"You don't know?"

Her hair stirred softly with a negative motion of her head. "I went to the bunkhouse to ask you again if you'd come to supper. You were gone and the crew said you and Bill Treat went to town together. Said they didn't know why . . . they sounded uneasy and evasive." Her ripe underlip formed a petulant shape. "Nobody tells me anything . . . always treating me like a child—"

"Now," Trevannon said quietly, "you'll have to act the woman. I'm in trouble, bad trouble."

Her eyes dilated darkly; she said swiftly, "Come in. Quick, before you're seen."

She moved back, and Trevannon wormed sideways between sash and sill, stepped inside. Andrea drew the shade down and turned to face him. "What is it, Wes?"

Trevannon breathed more easily; she was responding maturely and sensibly now. *But she changes like the wind,* he reminded himself, *so go easy.* He began to talk, studying her face closely, and as he spoke he saw her first resolution falter. Yet she said nothing, only stood unmoving, hardly breathing. Wes felt a cold uneasiness; the girl was a complete enigma—how would she react? Still he had to see out this thing he'd begun, and he kept talking, quietly and reasonably.

When he'd finished she said very softly, "But you can't just go away like this, Wes. What will I do?"

"I told you," Trevannon said patiently. "I gave you the facts about Treat and McQuayle. Use 'em."

"But Mother told me that Bill Treat will be foreman again," she said, half-whimpering. "That was just after you disappeared with Treat. I didn't understand then—but she sounded so smug, so sure—"

"Look, Andrea . . ." Trevannon drew a deep breath. "It sounds to me like your ma and Treat are dealing behind your back—listen to me, dammit!" he added savagely as her attention listlessly strayed. "You're mistress of Kaysee. Get that through your head! You got the say-so here; when you say cricket, they chirp. But you got to start believing it. Here's my advice. Get rid of Treat and make your peace with the Canaanites. They're good people and understanding, and you'll need friends like that—"

"But what about you?"

"I told you, the law's breathing on my neck. I'll be lucky to get shed of this valley a jump ahead of Jans Vandermeer. Bell's likely come to, roused him by now. And he won't wait. I got to cut out now, no choice. Girl, you got to brace up, face life like it is. For your sake, for your ma's—"

She seized on that straw. "Oh, but I can't trust her. She does things behind my back, you know that."

Wes nodded coldly. "She's part of what you'll have to handle—by yourself."

"But I can't run Kaysee!" she wailed.

"Gabe Morrow's a man can be trusted. Make him foreman, he'll handle the ranch end."

Andrea's slender shafts of argument were used up. She faced him mutely, her face deathly white. And Trevannon realized amazedly that she was frightened—actually terrified. This baffled him, till she moved closer and her hands reached blindly, caught his arms. She came against him, her head bowed on his chest. Her low voice was a muffled sound.

He bent his head. "What?"

"I said, I love you."

Trevannon felt the shock of it, was strongly aware of her firmly rounded body trembling against him like a scared child's, and the fragrance of her hair. A sum of heady temptation that he forced from him; he stepped back, his hands on her shoulders holding her at arm's length. Her tear-streaked face tilted up, and seeing it he felt only pity then and a deep sadness.

"Child, you don't know what you're saying."

Sudden anger sparked her violet eyes. She stamped her foot. "I do so! You're just like the rest—" she broke off with a tremulous smile. "Just like a man, too blind to see what's under his very nose. But you do understand now, don't you, Wes?"

"Sure," he said hollowly. "I understand."

A fierce joy blazed in her face. "Oh, good. That solves everything, don't you see? I only argued about those other things to make you stay. And you know why I really wanted you to stay. I don't give a damn about this silly old ranch or Mother either!" Her mouth twisted in a brief, ugly way. "I hate her. I'm tired of her nagging and her orders. If I stayed, it would only be more of the same." Again her bright eagerness. "But I don't have to stay, do I?—Not now."

"Look," Trevannon got out, "if you're thinking—"

"But certainly, darling. I'm going with you. See how simple it is?"

Trevannon shook his head slowly. "I can't be your father, Andrea."

"What *are* you talking about?" she said exasperatedly, and then laughed. "Wait till you learn what I can be, for you."

"I don't want to find out," he said doggedly. "That's what I'm telling you, girl. No good arguing about it." She raised her arms and came to him, but he caught her wrists and thrust her roughly away. "Now quit that! I'm leaving now, and you're staying here. Understand?"

She flinched from his harsh anger as from a slap, and a flush of abrupt rage beat into her face. Swiftly it mounted beyond rage, ugly and chilling. For Trevannon, there was something coldly familiar in the varnished blankness of her stare, and then he knew. He's seen it in Bodie Teece only a few days ago, that one state of mind with which nobody can argue. He stepped back to the window, warily watching her.

"You won't take me with you," she murmured tensely. "So you won't take me with you. Well, Tige will fix you. Tige!" She screamed the name. *"Tige, come here!"*

Trevannon slung his leg over the sill and ducked out, sprinting for the grove. He tore through it at a run, cut wide around the outbuildings to reach his horse. As he hit the saddle he looked back, saw a lantern bobbing from the bunkhouse as somebody exited on the run, headed for the main house. Faint screams still throbbed in his ears, and Trevannon found himself shaking, sickened by what he had witnessed. God alone knew how long it had been building in her, to this . . . a thing before which he, like all men, was powerless.

He could not help Andrea Carter. His thoughts veered to the Canaanites. Nothing left but to warn them of McQuayle. And there was Calla Waybeck; suddenly he wanted to be with her and be touched by her full serenity, the gentle reserve that glided over calm strength. He seized on that like a drowning man in a sea of shadows. Nothing else made sense any longer. This he could accept with relief, without question.

He turned roughly south for the Canaanite settlement. The night was black and moonless, and the stars were overcast, lending only a faint silvery complexion to the oceanic roll of grassland. He did not know this country well, and with landmarks and stars hidden, even his lifetime plainsman's instinct was baffled. It would be too easy to head wrong. And he needed rest and sleep badly. The strain of these last hours had been fierce; his head and body ached from the brutal beating Treat had administered.

Accordingly he pulled into the lee of an outcrop, hobbled the bay and settled himself into a crotch of rock, propped half upright with his gun in his lap. Sleepily he mapped out his future moves . . . catch a few hours' sleep and be on his way at first light. He'd lose no margin of safety, for the thick darkness would hold back pursuers till then. See the Canaanites and ride on from the valley without delay, as fast and far as possible. He felt a numb pang of regret, thinking of Calla. A hell of a time for two years of loneliness to catch up, he thought distantly, as if he hadn't enough barbs

working in his hide already. A minute later his exhausted
mind mercifully let go, and he slept like a log.

Kilrain Carter had had a fine oaken four-poster bed
freighted in before he'd brought his new bride to Kaysee a
year ago. She had been tense and frightened that first night:
this was one thing for which her mother hadn't prepared her.
And it had been fully as terrible as she'd expected, for
Kilrain Carter was never a gentle man, with men or horses
or with a woman, and finally he had turned in disgust from
her pain and fear and sobbing. Later it hadn't been so bad,
but the sick knowledge that she was only a plaything for an
aging man's last brittle fling at lust had stayed with her.
She'd found relief in his masculine domination, except
for this shameful stain that she couldn't wipe from
memory. . . .

It kept coming back to Andrea now as she lay alone in her
vast bed, while the dreary, pre-dawn light filtered through
the east window. But the remembrance was muddy and
inchoate, broken by other thoughts which moved in and out
of her mind like patches of light and shadow. Her head hurt
so that she wanted to scream aloud. But she only lay quietly,
wide eyes fixed on the gray frame of ceiling, her bosom
hardly stirring with her breathing. Vaguely it occurred to her
once or twice that every warped circumstance of her life
was funneling at last into a breaking point, but this single
thrust toward sanity, like a warning bell in her mind,
flickered and drifted and was lost in her tattered thoughts.

Suddenly she began to shiver uncontrollably though the
graying darkness was warm and close, and she clutched the
blankets to her, feeling small and lost and afraid. If only
Trevannon had not left her. For a moment her thoughts held
warmly on the tall man, and she was sorry she had sent Tige
after him. Then she thought spitefully, *He had it coming.
Leaving me all alone. I hope Tige hurts him good.* Anyway,
she still had Mother. *Oh, no,* she thought with abrupt stark
hatred, *it was all Mother's fault.* Strangely she was no

longer sure exactly how, but only that her mother was somehow to blame. . . .

She did remember clearly how her outcries had brought the crew boiling over to the main house in a body, with Tige Menefee loping in the lead. She had met them on the veranda and screamed at them, "What are you staring at? Go on, get back to the bunkhouse, all of you—no, Tige, stay here." She remembered their startled, sleep-drugged stares, and then they had filed sheepishly back to the bunkhouse, except for Menefee. Still trembling with anger, she had given him his orders in a low, strangled hiss. Tige had responded instantly, without surprise or question; he'd nodded and was gone in the night.

Andrea had turned back into the dark parlor to hear her mother's voice calling for an explanation. In the darkness Andrea had reached out and grasped the empty wheel chair, and its hard feel had steadied her. She'd even smiled then. Nightly she helped her mother to bed, leaving the wheel chair in the parlor. Her mother insisted on this, to enforce obedience . . . but she could not leave her bed without help. *"Andrea, Andrea, you wicked girl, come here at once!"* And Andrea had only stood, smiling and listening, as the peremptory tone became an imploring wail . . . finally died into silence.

Andrea had returned quietly to her room. But sleep had not come. The stillness grew oppressive . . . frightening. It was all very well to make this token rejection of her mother, but Kilrain was gone, Trevannon was gone, Daddy was gone, and there was no one to turn to but Mother.

Dimly now, she knew that hours had gone by as she lay there; her fists clenched in the folds of the coverlet. *No no no, I hate her! I won't go back to her, I won't!* The core of pain swelled till she thought her head would burst, and she couldn't lie still any longer.

She flung herself out of bed and ran to the commode, fumbling blindly for the lamp there. She found a match and lifted the sooted chimney. Her hands were trembling wildly and after she struck the match she could not steady it to the wick. Desperately she clasped the lamp to her breast and bit her lip intently as she lighted the wick. At that moment the match scorched her fingers, and she cried out and flung the lamp from her to nurse her thumb.

The lamp hit the floor and broke, sending a spray of coal oil across the carpet. It caught at once, a sheet of flame whipping along the floor. "Oh," Andrea said aloud, "I've got to stop it." She began to stoop and pick up an edge of the carpet; she straightened, watching wide-eyed the progress of the flames as they licked avidly at the log walls.

She would not stop the fire, and it would serve Mother right. The thought began as a momentary and shocking impulse, against which she briefly recoiled. But as she continued to watch the out-fanning flames with fascination, it came back forcefully, and with it a great sense of relief. The tension and fear vanished, and she laughed joyfully aloud. She let her nightgown slip to the floor and paused, liking the sensual glow of rosy heat against her body. But she would have to leave the house now. Almost reluctantly she began to dress. Her movements were automatic; her mind danced like a gay moth, glorying in this forbidden fruit.

Dressed, she ran from the house with her hair streaming out behind. Reached the narrow areaway between the carriage house and a tool shed, sank breathlessly down between the walls. She watched awhile as the flames tongued through the windows and peeled up the outside walls, mounting swiftly to the roof. The logs were old and almost tinder-dry, and the whole east wing had caught now. Mother usually slept the sleep of the dead. Andrea grinned at the thought, hugging her knees and rocking back and forth.

It seemed a long time before the loudening crackle of the fire brought a faint shout from the bunkhouse. Soon the dark shapes of men were pounding past her shelter, and she scrooched deeper into the shadows, making herself small between the shed walls. If she were found she would be punished, and she didn't want that. Once at Doctor Mack's, she had got a whole box of lucifers off the pantry shelf and set them afire. *"Andrea, you naughty girl! Do you want to burn down the house?"* *"But the fire is so pretty, and I made it for you, Mama."* Andrea bit her thumb gleefully, watching a roaring torrent of flame belch across the dry roof shakes. *If only Daddy could see the fire, too.*

The shouts of the men forming a bucket line to the creek hurt her ears, and the leaping flames hurt her eyes; she rubbed grimy knuckles against her lids and looked away. She did not remember Daddy very well. He was a thin, tired man in bib overalls, and Mommy called him Curt . . . or no, was that someone else? Maybe Daddy was the big, gray-haired man with the silvery wheels on the band on his black hat . . . Kilrain. There was another man mixed in somewhere too, a tall, homely man with yellow hair who had left her alone, and try as she might, she couldn't remember his name at all. Anyway, they were all gone now, all except Mama.

"Where are you, Mama?" she whimpered, beginning to feel afraid again. Only the crackle of flames answered her. She felt sleepy and confused and scared, and here she was all alone, and it wasn't fair. Maybe . . . if you could go back and start all over again, maybe you could make it come out right. If you could go way down deep into the darkness where it all began, you could start over. Why, that was the answer, she thought excitedly. And she was not at all surprised that she knew; it seemed that she'd always known.

She got to her feet and slipped out at the back of the areaway, running to the shed for her bridle, and then to the corral for her black horse. She did this without thinking about it. All the men were fighting the fire on the far side of the ranch layout, and nobody saw her leave.

CHAPTER 14

TREVANNON HAD ALWAYS HAD THE LUCKY FACULTY OF clockwork slumber, waking almost to a minute of his choosing. He came awake and alert all at once, and though it seemed he'd dozed off minutes ago, he saw gray false dawn now belting the eastern sky, picking out the land in shadowy outline . . . time to travel.

He rode straight northeast, retracing the route he'd followed two days ago. He hit a branch of the creek and followed it for a time, forded it at a shallow crossing, and shortly left the rich grasslands of Kaysee open range for the scrubby country to the east, where ridge and flatland, meadow and forest, merged helter-skelter.

The first pink flush of true dawn was dissipating the last murkiness when he left a belt of timber and headed across a badly eroded roll of flats, with its scalped hummocks and deep-worn gullies. . . .

He felt the heavy thud of a long rifle slug slam sickeningly into the bay's flank behind the left forehock. Felt the beast's convulsive dying shudder beneath him even as the rifle's bark whipcracked brittle echoes across the clear, still air.

As the bay's weight sloughed sideways, he kicked from the stirrups and left the saddle, saw the brown earth cant wildly toward him, and lit on his shoulder and hip with a grinding impact that drove the breath from his body. He rolled in blind panic from the falling horse and stopped face-down when he heard the hard cantle crunch against the ground. He got his hands beneath him and pushed his body a foot upward before the second shot thudded into the horse. It twitched with a final muscular spasm, and was still. Trevannon flattened out again as two more shots came, one laid so near it flung dust against his legs.

He squirmed around on his belly and floundered an awkward yard to the shelter of his dead mount. He hugged the saddle and rump with his body, buried his face in the mane. The rifleman deliberately and unhurriedly sent three more shots into the carcass, held fire then.

Five minutes dragged by and Trevannon did not move, his heart thudding painfully against his cramped ribs. He had caught only a confused glimpse of powder smoke laying a pale smudge against the dark lift of timber high on a looming ridge off to his right. A fact of no value whatever. Even if the ambusher weren't completely hidden, he was out of pistol range, and Trevannon's saddle boot was empty; Treat had taken his rifle. Here he was nailed securely, pocketed precariously behind an inert carcass. For ten feet in any direction was no other cover. He might make it to his feet, but he'd be a dead man before he took a second step. . . .

This he knew from the deadly accuracy with which the first bullet had been placed, directly to the bay's heart. Baffled ignorance of the rifleman's identity was an added goad to his sense of utter helplessness. He gripped hard on his nerves then and reasoned three things: the man was full of unrelenting hatred, enough to play cat-and-rat with a certain victim; he had iron, self-possessed patience that had enabled him to wait till he could drop his victim in this open trap; he was an uncanny woodsman who could trail in bad light, follow unseen while matching Trevannon's own pace, and even work ahead of his quarry to pick a likely spot.

For Trevannon had no doubt that this deadfall was by anything but chance; he'd left all his enemies behind. One had followed. . . .

He took off his hat, raised his head till his eyes just

cleared shelter, straining his vision against the black timber. He caught a flicker of neutral color which moved, became a horse and rider shifting across a break in the timber. He recognized Tige Menefee's big blue mustang and the half-breed's easy saddle slouch, before the trees swallowed him a second later. Tige was working downhill, coming in closer. Trevannon held his breath, wondering if this might not be the time to run. He got a knee under him and half-rose and was answered by the instant crash of the rifle. He dived flat again, his sweating face pressed to the dirt.

Tige Menefee . . . of course. Tige, seething with all the jealous, single-minded hatred of his savage blood . . . set on his trail by the girl Menefee blindly worshipped. A girl who'd strike out in the only way she knew . . . like a hurt child, without thought, without regard for the consequences. And Tige would play this dragged-out game which could have only one end to the last drop of torment he could wring from his prey.

Trevannon twisted on his belly, eyeing longingly a patch of trees fifty feet to his right. If he could achieve that, he could work around into the timber cover of the ridge. There he could move freely on somewhat equal terms, where Tige's rifle would give him no edge.

A morning breeze rose off the flats and whipped along the level ground, stirring the long hair which had fallen lankly over his forehead. He tossed it back out of his face and gripped the dusty sod in his frustration, twisting the sere grass in his hands.

Wind and grass . . . *fire!* The idea grenaded into his consciousness. He tore a handful of the dry graze from its weak rooting. The breeze was strengthening, blowing toward the ridge. Erosion had done its dirty work here, and a dry summer had finished the job. A stretch of dead grass rolled sparsely to the foot of the ridge. Enough of it to carry a line of fire to the dying brush that heavily mantled the lower ridge.

He began tearing up all the grass within his reach, fisting a half-dozen bunches around small pebbles for weight. Tige had now settled into a fresh position, and he laid a few desultory shots fairly close, evidently amusing himself. Trevannon unbuttoned the breast pocket of his jacket to get out an oilcloth-wrapped packet of matches which he laid out by the grass bunches. Methodically he struck a match and touched it to each bunch, the dry blades flaring at once with a clean hot blaze. He squirmed onto his back and tossed them out one by one, roughly spacing his throws across a line thirty feet long. Then he flattened hard against the ground and the carcass, knowing that Tige would now begin firing in earnest.

Menefee pumped his magazine empty with a haste that told of his first alarm that his quarry might escape. Bullets hammered into the horse, into the earth, scattering dust and pebbles over Trevannon's clothes. The half-breed's long pause to reload . . . while crawling flames spread and joined into a blazing line which ate toward the ridge. Fine banners of smoke wisped up, not yet enough to lend cover.

And then, as Tige resumed firing, the flames reached the first tangles of vine-covered brush and crackled avidly upward with a terrifying speed. Masses of vegetation exploded into fireballs; where dead brush merged with green wood, dark smoke billowed thickly and was windborne up the ridge face. Menefee was in sudden danger, and Trevannon heard his racked coughing and afterward the crash of brush as he plunged up the slope.

Trevannon lunged to his feet, long legs driving him toward that clump of timber. Hit the fringe of trees and kept running, cutting a semi-circle to come up on the flank of the ridge. He heard Tige's mettlesome, half-broken blue, panicked at the first smell of smoke, come bursting blindly through the heavy brush straight for him. Trevannon breasted the brush savagely, his hard-driven breath searing his lungs, to head off the blue.

He plunged into a small clearing and across it as the blue came tearing through the last impeding undergrowth. Wes leaped in recklessly to grab for its bridle. He caught it as the startled brute reared, then pivoted to avoid the flailing hoofs. He iron-handed the brute down and got astride with a leaping twist of his body before it could wheel to avoid him.

The mustang fought, piledriving savagely, with Trevannon's spine catching every crushing downjolt. He knew a bleak flash of horseman's admiration for Menefee, whose uncanny sense for horseflesh had mastered this surging power so easily.

And Menefee was coming; Trevannon heard his loping bounds through the underbrush. Tige could hear the struggle but must have mistaken its real nature, for he whistled shrilly. Amazingly and at once the blue stopped fighting; his laid-back ears pricked up and he only snorted and sidled uneasily beneath his alien rider.

At the same time Menefee plowed through the last growth, his head bent behind his flailing arms. Trevannon knew sinkingly that now there would be no avoiding a showdown, as he'd hoped; he slid out his Colt as Menefee broke into the clearing.

The breed's inky eyes flared with the upswing of his head, absorbing the situation in an instant. He whipped up the rifle across his body, bringing it to bear . . . too late, for Trevannon's pistol was already trained. But the half-breed's sudden movement set off the blue again; he careened wildly as Trevannon fired—missed. Tige brought the rifle to his shoulder, sighting carefully to get Trevannon's jolting body in his sights.

And Trevannon clamped a tight and desperate rein on the blue, halting its gyrations for a breath-held instant. The barrel of his six-gun was still braced over the lifted forearm of his bridle-hand. Almost without aiming, he shot.

The shots crashed as one. A smashing blow drove Trevannon sideways from the saddle, and he jerked stirrup-free by instinct, hit the ground rolling and stopped face-down and stunned. He heard the blue bolt from the clearing. Only a powerful effort of panicked will enabled him to roll on his side to face Menefee, wildly wondering why the breed hadn't shot again. . . .

Tige lay on his back with his legs jackknifed grotesquely,

his side-tilted head fixing his sightless stare on Trevannon. The pointblank slug had taken him chest-center. Wes dropped his head into the dirt and closed his eyes, fighting back the black, dizzy waves that engulfed him. Only the blazing pain reaching through the blackness forced him throbbingly awake.

He was hit on the same side where he had caught Kittredge's try a few days ago, but this time it was deep, it was bad; and he knew he must summon strength to move, else die where he was.

Strangling whiffs of smoke, the crackle of flames, warned him that the inferno he'd begun would catch him in its path within minutes. Thus goaded, he pushed himself up on his hands and knees, and then to his feet. He stumbled with slack, dragging steps from the clearing and headed down-ridge.

At the bottom he fell to his knees. Took a few panting seconds to muster fresh strength, feeling the hot wetness plaster across his back and soak his pants. He frowned and focused his rambling thoughts. Ah . . . he hadn't been more than a half-mile from the Canaanite settlement when he ran into this deadfall. It was just beyond the next ridge, outlined by black jagged pinecrests. Surely someone had heard the shooting and would investigate.

But he could not wait, and he tried to stand again—failed. He began to crawl, pausing each few shuffling feet and reaching doggedly for the waning will that would take him a little farther.

CHAPTER 15

IN CASSIUS MCQUAYLE'S SHABBY OFFICE, BILL TREAT SAT with his legs outstretched, staring unseeingly at the slat of early sunlight streaming through the musty window across his cracked boots. His bull head was sunk on his great chest, hands rammed in his pockets, and his eyes brooded sullenly. He scarcely heard Cassius McQuayle's frightened berating of him.

"You utter fool," McQuayle muttered as he frenziedly paced the floor. "Why in hell did I listen to you! Damn your—"

"Enough from you, old man," Treat said heavily, raising his head. His eyes, red-rimmed from lack of sleep, the cold fear that sat him now like an icy hand, made his glance very ugly. "You were ready to tie in with my idea when it looked sure-fire. Now we hit a snag, you ain't backin' out."

McQuayle subsided into his swivel chair, muttering, "All the same, if that boy lives to talk— It was your doing, not mine."

Treat grinned coldly. "Ain't they some shyster lingo to cover that—like accessory before the fact? Man, you're in it to your neck. Take it a step further—suppose Bell lives long enough to talk, then dies? That'd mean the noose for me, not much better for you. You're an old, sick man, Cass; prison 'd finish you in short order."

"And if you're nailed for murder," McQuayle whispered, "you'd incriminate me—out of pure spite?"

"Man, that's rank injustice. Wouldn't tell on no one who plays square with me. Thing is"—Treat hunched forward in his chair, gently shaking a meaty finger—"there's no reason either of us should stay around to git caught. Yonder's twenty thousand dollars Vandermeer left stashed in your safe, plus what you was savin' to buy that land off the Canaanites. Enough to take us a hell of a way, buy a sight of good livin' when we get there."

McQuayle picked up his tobacco plug, tore off a chunk with his teeth and crammed it in the pouch of his cheek. He chewed wildly, muttering, "I have a bad heart—can't set a fugitive's pace. And a steal that size will get every lawman in the territory and beyond posted on our descriptions."

"A long shot," Treat agreed. "But it's that or rot in prison for you—hangin' for me. Think it over."

Treat grimly watched McQuayle's scrawny frame seeming to shrink into itself, growing even smaller, and was silent then to let this sink in. . . .

It had seemed so easy, so foolproof last night when the prospect of wealth and fulfilled desires had dazzled Treat into the certainty that Trevannon's mouth must be shut for good. All he had to do was wait till the town was asleep, steal into the alleyway by the jail, stick a gun through the barred window and pull the trigger. A pleasant job done for the price of a bullet, as he'd told McQuayle.

He had gone to the jail shortly after midnight. By standing on tiptoe he was able to angle his vision down into the cell, where a blanket-covered form lay huddled face down on the narrow cot, dimly illuminated by a lantern hanging in the corridor beyond. Good . . . no witnesses, for the man in the other cell was sleeping off a drunk. As he watched, Trevannon had twitched fitfully beneath the blanket and feebly moaned; seeing his enemy's nerve shattered had pleased Treat immensely.

As he'd brought his gun up to the bars and cocked it, he couldn't resist saying aloud, "Man, don't be sad. Here's to endin' your misery." At the sound of his voice the cot's occupant had twisted wildly, and then Treat fired. Saw to his frozen horror that it wasn't Trevannon at all, as the man rolled on his side and he stared into the putty-white face of Job Bell. The deputy strained to sit up, and the blanket fell away. He clutched at his chest and then rolled sideways off the cot, crumpling limply on the floor. The drunk was aroused by the shot, mumbling, "What 'a hell? What 'a hell?"

The sights and sounds of those few seconds were compressed in Treat's brain with crystal clarity. He'd snapped to his senses then and melted swiftly back into the shadows, pounding along the rear of buildings with unreasoning terror lending wings to his feet. Again and again, during the hours since, he'd cursed himself for leaving the mistaken shooting half-finished; he could have made sure of Bell. In his scared confusion, he'd thought only of flight.

He'd figured it out by now: Trevannon had somehow tricked Bell, knocked him cold, and escaped. Bell had been coming to when Treat had arrived. Lord, if he had only waited till Bell turned his face before he fired. . . . *If—if!* he thought savagely; it was done, and he had to apply his wit to getting out of this with a whole skin . . . had to size up every angle, weigh each with care. Bell had surely recognized his voice, had probably made out his face at the window before he passed out. Bell, if he lived, could pinpoint the man who'd shot him. . . .

When he'd got his trembling panic under control, Treat had hurried to the doctor's house at the end of town. A small crowd was already gathering, including an elderly couple who were Job Bell's parents. And Jans Vandermeer was there, his face rock-grim, wearing only his pants over his woolen underwear. Treat learned that the sheriff, who was staying with Job and his family, had left his bed on the run at the sound of the shot, expecting that one of the Kaysee crowd might have tried to break Trevannon out. Finding his deputy unconscious and bleeding on the floor confirmed his suspicion. Treat had never seen the sheriff's mountainous calm so shattered; his broad face was pale and tight, and his huge fists kept closing and unclosing; he plainly had the thinnest grip on his boiling fury.

Vandermeer had turned to Job's father, who wore a dazed expression as he tried automatically to comfort his weeping wife. "John, you had better take Mrs. Bell home. It will be very bad, the next few hours. . . . And the rest of you leave now. Go back to your homes. No, you stay, Bill."

Treat had wondered with a stab of fear what Vandermeer wanted with him as the onlookers cleared out of the doctor's little waiting room. When the two of them were alone, Vandermeer's final shred of calm had broken. He'd swiped savagely at the air with his fist; his voice shook. "God, Bill, I must be getting old. I am fond of that boy; I was grooming him to fill my boots. Job had much to learn. Ah, Lord, why did I leave him alone with that clever devil?"

"Too hard on yourself, Dutchy," Treat had said uneasily. "How is the kid?"

Vandermeer had jerked a nod toward the closed door to the adjoining room. "Doctor Griffith cannot tell yet; he is now removing the bullet. It went in just under the heart. He must live, Bill; that boy must live. Yet, I'm afraid. . . ."

Treat had weakly cleared his throat. "Ah, you wanted to talk to me—"

"Yes," Vandermeer had said heavily. "You know Trevannon a little. The man is a riddle to me; yet I had not thought this of him. How does his mind work? Where will he go now—what will he do?"

Carefully hiding his vast relief, Treat had given a wry shrug. "Your guess is damned near as good as mine. Still—" Treat had frowned thoughtfully. "Heres a hunch you can play for what it's worth. Mrs. Congreve told me Trevannon was over visitin' them Canaanites—got right friendly with the clan, so she says. Stuck up for 'em agin Kaysee. Now he knows you'd look for him first at Kaysee—he wouldn't stop there. So—"

"Wait, Bill," Vandermeer had scowled impatiently. "I have visited the Canaanites on my rounds. They are fine people, the only ones I can be sure will never make trouble. Ephraim Waybeck is my good friend, the salt of the earth. These people would not harbor criminals. Nor would such a man as this befriend them. Mrs. Congreve was surely mistaken."

Treat's sly thoughts were now functioning swiftly. "Possible. But like you said—that Trevannon's a tough nut to crack; no telling how his mind works. Told you before how he charmed hisself into that foreman's job. Likely he had some reason of his own for makin' up to the Canaanites. And, not meanin' to slight old Waybeck, he is a kinda simple soul. . . . Trevannon'll have one neat story for him, puttin' himself in the right, the law in the wrong. You'll look like a damn ogre before he's finished. And he'll figure like you just did—that the Canaanite settlement is the last place you'd look. Even if you show up, they'll hide him, cover for him. Yessir," Treat finished emphatically, "that's the place to look, mark me."

The sheriff had smiled thinly. "I have always admired your thinking, Bill—if not your tactics so much. Such as throwing the Canaanites off their homesteads."

Treat shrugged. "Took my orders from Kilrain Carter, like always. Anyway . . . they didn't complain, did they?"

"No," Vandermeer said wearily, "they did not complain. Luckily their lack of respect for the law in no way impairs their observance of it." His face hardened again. "I will see them now. If they think to hide Trevannon—they will learn that this was a mistake."

"Man, it's pitch dark." Treat added mildly. "That's why I didn't go back to Kaysee tonight myself."

"Still, I should be able to hold the wagon road as far as Kaysee; I will make certain that Trevannon did not return to the ranch. By then it will be light enough to cut across-country to the Canaanites'." He went on brusquely, being first and always a man of the law, "I cannot wait to learn news of Job. Perhaps then you will do the goodness to wait and follow me later with news of the boy."

When he'd gone, Treat hung around the waiting room, pacing restlessly, staring at that blank hardwood door till the tension threatened to crack his nerves. When he could stand it no longer, he rapped on a panel. "Doc!"

Dr. Griffith had opened the door a crack, his bushy gray hair awry. "Damn it, Treat. I'm fighting for a man's life in here. If you can't pry yourself away, at least keep quiet!"

"He ain't—?"

"I've removed the bullet; he has a fighting chance."

"Dutchy's gone after the killer," Treat had said hastily. "If the kid comes to, I'm supposed to get word—"

"I'll let you know if he does," the doctor had retorted waspishly, and had shut the door.

Treat had remained there in an agony of suspense, afraid that Job's first words on reviving would be to breathe the name of his attacker. John Bell came in several times to ask news of his son, then hurried home to take care of his wife. By sunup, Treat's patience had frayed out . . . also he wanted to make sure of McQuayle. He'd tramped up to the lawyer's office to find him in a funk of pure fright. McQuayle had learned from a citizen what had happened, and was afterward too terrified to leave his office.

Talking to McQuayle had eased Treat's tension enough to let his mind function freely. He hadn't quite dared to consider his next step if Job should talk. Now he did, grimly and methodically.

McQuayle broke the long quiet, his voice taut and shrill. "All right, Bill. I've thought it over; you're right, of course. But may I inquire what in hell you are waiting for? The sooner we leave, the better."

"Old man, shut your mouth, eh? We'll break when I say so, not before."

The distinct wicked edge to it shut McQuayle up. Treat shifted his glowering attention back to his boots. He could not bring himself to accept that his blunder might have wiped out all his grandiose dreams of a few hours ago. If he broke and ran now, only to learn later that Job Bell had died without talking, he'd have thrown away everything for nothing. This possibility gnawed at his insides. He couldn't abandon the fight till he was certain he'd lost. Whatever he had to do, Vandermeer was out of the way for the time being—that was a break.

With his grim course mentally set, he rose and left the office. McQuayle called after him; he didn't reply or glance back. He hit the street, went up the block and turned onto the sidestreet where Dr. Griffith had his house and business.

Treat entered the waiting room and found it still deserted. He seated himself with automaton stiffness on a sagging couch, dangled his hat between his fingers and stared at the far wall. Long ago, when he was young and reckless, he'd done a stint as teamster for a mining company. He remembered how once, driving a loaded ore wagon with a ten-mule-span hitch down a narrow, twisting road, his brake handle had snapped off short. He felt now the same detached numbness, that of a man caught on a careening vehicle gone out of control on a mountainside, and nothing to do but ride it out clear to the bottom. . . .

The door to the side room opened. Treat steadied down on his raw nerves and met the doctor's tired gaze calmly as the medico stepped out, holding the door open.

"He's awake," Griffith said. "Weak—can't speak above a whisper. Seems to be rational, though. Keeps asking for the sheriff. . . ."

Treat moistened his lips. "Dutchy ain't back."

"Then you can talk to the boy . . . take his message. His condition is still critical, and he needs rest. He won't sleep till he gets this thing off his chest."

Treat nodded as he stood, saying softly, "After you, Doc."

He followed Griffith into the room, was careful to close the door tightly behind them. Bell lay on the narrow operating table with his bony upper body swathed in bandages. His young face was palely drawn; his breath whistled noisily in and out.

"Job," Doctor Griffith said gently.

Job painfully turned his head a little. As his gaze lighted on Treat, his body heaved spasmodically. Griffith caught him by the shoulders and held him down. "Easy, boy . . . for God's sake, easy."

"Doc," Job whispered harshly. "He's the one . . . Treat. One who shot me."

Griffith frowned. "No, Job. Try to think clearly. Don't make a mistaken accusation that could hurt an innocent man. Think back . . . it was another man who shot you. Who was he?"

"Doc . . . got to believe me. Treat . . . was Treat. Trevannon . . . only knocked me out. Come to . . . heard Treat's voice . . . saw his face . . . window. Shot me. . . ."

Job's whisper waned and his eyes flickered and closed. Griffith straightened slowly, removed his glasses and tucked them into his breast pocket as he turned frowningly toward Treat—then stiffened at sight of the gun in the stocky man's fist.

"So you did—"

"Turn around, Doc," Treat said huskily. The doctor did not move, and Treat rasped, "I said turn, damn you!" He grabbed the slender physician by the shoulder and savagely spun him about. Whipped the gun barrel up and down. Dr. Griffith wilted to the floor.

For a long moment Treat intently regarded the man on the table, listening to his harsh breathing. Thinking bitterly, *Sounds like he ain't got long. But Doc knows, damn him!* He looked down at the crumpled medico, and for an instant the wild impulse chased through his mind to shoot, wipe out the valid witness. His thumb eared the gun-hammer to full cock.

But he did not even point it, as the madness of the notion

bore fully home on him. A shot would bring people. Even could he dispose of these two quietly, there'd be others who'd seen him enter the house. And this killing could not be blamed on Trevannon. Too, Trevannon, if he were caught, could give an explanation that would point a convincing finger straight at Bill Treat. And McQuayle would certainly break wide open, admit everything to save his own hide. With all odds stacked against him, there was one way open: flight.

He stirred the limp form of Griffith with his foot; satisfied that the doctor would be out long enough to give him a good start, he let his gun off-cock, sheathed it, and left, headed back to McQuayle's office.

The old con man was hunched against his desk, his face buried in his hands. He came erect as Treat entered and slammed the door. "Bill, what—"

"Bell talked," Treat said tersely. "I laid the Doc out cold. There's time to use. Open that safe. We got to move fast."

McQuayle sat frozen. Treat, out of patience, stalked to the desk, grabbed him by the collar and yanked him to his feet. "Get a hold on yourself, you old fool, and *open that safe!*"

As he spoke, he threw McQuayle stumbling away, and the lawyer's frail form hit solidly against the safe edge. He bowed forward and collapsed across it. Without a sound he rolled slackly sideways and crumpled to the floor.

Treat didn't believe it. He went down on his knees, turned the body over. McQuayle's head lolled back, his mouth fallen open. His wide-blank eyes were sightless.

His goddamn heart! Treat climbed to his feet with a stiff, mechanical effort, his eyes dragging to the safe. Twenty thousand-some dollars a foot away . . . and it might as well have been in China. He thought of rifling McQuayle's desk—the combination might be written down some-where—and knew, even as the thought occurred to him, that McQuayle wouldn't be so careless.

The room tilted dizzily, as though the walls were closing on him. He steadied quickly. Yet in that moment something died hard in Bill Treat, and he forgot about Andrea Carter and Kaysee and twenty thousand dollars. He knew one elemental urge now, to live, beat his way out of a trap, get far away. . . .

He ran from the office, half fell down the stairwell to get outside. His horse was tied at the rail in readiness. He ripped free the reins, vaulted on and kicked into a crazy run.

He'd head eastward, over the mountains; he knew an easy pass out of the valley. He'd stop at Kaysee only long enough to pick up his belongings. Beyond that he had no idea what would happen, and just now, quirting his horse viciously to greater speed, he did not care.

Treat dropped the reins of his lathered, shuddering horse, and took a dazed step toward the smoldering wreckage of the house. Charred timbers projected like black, smoking jackstraws from its collapsed ruin. He was hardly aware of the crewmen standing about, their clothes scorched and sooted, nursing their burns, apathetic after their failure to save the house.

"Looks like you damn close to killed that horse." This cold disapproval from Gabe Morrow.

Treat didn't answer. Something like a sob broke in his thick chest. This house, center of the great ranch that was a sacred monument in his mind . . . the house he'd shared with old Kilrain for years before the Old Man had brought his bride to Kaysee. Burned to the ground, gone forever. It was the crowning blow to all that had happened; it even diverted Treat's rage to get away into a sudden venom of explosive hatred.

"Who done it?"

"Can't say how it started," Gabe muttered dispiritedly. "It was caught on too good by the time we roused out. Couldn't hardly get close enough to toss water, for the heat.

Couple of us tried to git in, git the women out; damn near got burned up before we reached the door, couldn't make it. . . . The old lady couldn't walk, but can't figure why Mrs. Carter didn't clear out. Smoke must've overcome 'em both. . . ." Gabe's voice trailed off, and he shook his head back and forth, back and forth.

"Who done it?" Treat asked again.

"Bill, I tol' you— Where'n hell you going?"

Treat had turned back to his jaded horse. He led it to the corral and stripped off saddle and bridle. Then he plodded doggedly to the bunkhouse, jammed his few belongings in his warsack, and tramped back to the corral. He saddled a rangy, strong-winded pinto and fastened on his warsack. All this he did very methodically, and he rode away from Kaysee headquarters for the last time without looking back.

Treat knew exactly what he was going to do, and hell or high water couldn't stop him. Of course it was Wes Trevannon who'd fired the house. He, Treat, was Kaysee; and Trevannon would pause in his flight to hurt Kaysee out of pure spite. He didn't ask himself whether this explanation made sense. As for Andrea, his reaction was one less of grief than of thwarted fury. Why, dammit, everything that had gone wrong was Trevannon's doing. He seethed over that with a sense of almost joyful relief. Sure as hell . . . if Trevannon hadn't shown up at Kaysee and taken his job, he wouldn't have been drawn on, step by step, to this bind in which he was helplessly caught.

He rode southeast through the bright morning. Ahead lay the Canaanite settlement; directly beyond, the pass he'd follow out of the valley. He wouldn't even have to ride out of his way . . . just pay a brief visit. He hadn't been shamming when he'd told Jans Vandermeer his belief that Trevannon would look for sanctuary with the Canaanites. It figured, all right . . . and if he ran into Vandermeer there—with the death of Bell already scored against him— why stop with Trevannon? Besides, that damned lawman would be a positive danger, one he'd breathe easier for cutting down. . . . Yessir, it was figuring better now, straight as a bullet. Treat found the rough imagery amusing; he chuckled aloud. Straight as a bullet.

CHAPTER 16

TREVANNON CAME AWAKE SEVERAL TIMES, FIRST, TO FIND himself jogging painfully in an improvised litter made of a ragged greatcoat and two unpeeled poles . . . and then he passed out. He woke next to find himself face down with someone cleaning the wound in his back, his arms and legs thrashing, and himself bellowing in pain; strong hands pinned him back, and he fainted.

The third time he came to, very drowsily and with his shoulder throbbing, he turned his head with an effort to see a window with full dawn staining the sky, and the nimbus of Calla Waybeck's fair hair against it. Knew he wasn't dreaming when her cool fingers touched his face; he smiled and closed his eyes. Slept like the dead. Later on he had the impression that he was being moved, but knew when he woke that he must have dreamed it. . . .

He was lying belly down in the same wooden bunk where he'd last found himself. The single room of the Waybeck cabin was flooded with daylight, and he wondered at once how long he'd slept. He felt a good deal better, only slightly feverish. Though when he tried to move, he found himself weak as a half-drowned cat.

A warm pillow of savory cooking smells hit his face, and he saw Calla bent by the fireplace, as he'd first seen her. And the old woman was there, rocking gently to and fro, looking at him steadily without seeing him. Trevannon lay motionless, letting the pleasant sights and sounds and smells of this room wash gently through his consciousness, let its workaday bustle flood him with peace. . . .

The boy Jerry was sitting at the table, his chin in his hand and tow hair tumbling into his eyes as he frowned over a school primer. He tossed his hair back with a twist of his head, and his gaze widened on Trevannon watching him.

"The man's awake," he said softly.

Calla turned quickly from the fireplace and came to the bunk with her strong, lithe stride.

"Hello," Trevannon said weakly.

She nodded hello, smiling a little as she wiped her hands on her apron. She turned her head to call, "Grandpa," and then gave Wes an oddly tender attention.

Ephraim Waybeck bulked through the open doorway, his venerable face showing only kindly pleasure as he came to stand by Calla. "Well," he boomed gently, "and how is our guest feeling?"

"Hungry," Trevannon whispered. "Curious. Hungry first."

"You Texans are indeed a whang-leather breed," smiled Ephraim. "In spite of which, I think that a nourishing liquid is your limit at present. A bowl of broth, Calla. . . . The wound was not as serious as I first thought. When Elia and I found you, you were unconscious—I should say, from shock and blood-loss. A few days' rest will set you up."

"Haven't got . . . few days. Got to ride. . . ."

Ephraim squatted down, elbows on knees, his big, dirt-soiled hands laced loosely together. "That is out of the question, friend," he said seriously. "Though I hardly blame you, considering . . ."

"How much . . . you know?"

"Quite a little. Not enough." Ephraim's falcon eyes were speculative. "Here is what happened. . . ."

The Canaanites had been up before dawn, as was their custom; the men were already in the fields when they heard the shots and saw the smoke of the burning ridge. Ephraim and Elia had hurried to cover the half-mile on foot. They had found Trevannon unconscious near the base of the ridge, his dead horse nearby. When they had rigged a crude litter and borne Wes to the settlement, Ephraim had sent men back to fight the fire. As the land surrounding the ridge was mostly denuded, they'd easily halted the holocaust by scooping out a few trenches, letting the fire burn itself out on the ridge timber. As Ephraim had guessed that whoever had shot Trevannon might be on his trail, he'd also given orders to have the dead horse dragged off a distance and covered with brush.

"How effectively this might throw off your enemies, I did not know, but should they come, we could not defend you with guns; our only hope was to hide you, erase what sign we could." He paused somberly. "Unless I read you very wrongly the first time, I need not ask you to tell me nothing but the truth."

"Anything I can tell you," Trevannon husked gratefully.

Ephraim smiled and gripped his arm gently. "I know. First, what sign I could make out indicated that you had been shot at from ambush—that you started the fire to thwart your enemy. Who was he?"

Trevannon told him about Tige Menefee, weakly concluding, "His body was on the ridge . . . fire went over it, why you didn't find it . . . and his horse stampeded."

"I understand. How strong do you feel, sir? Strong enough to accept something of—bad news?" At Trevannon's nod of assent, Ephraim said, "I had no sooner finished removing the bullet, cleansing and bandaging your wound, when a horseman came across the Bench at a gallop. At once I anticipated your enemy."

He shifted aside to make room for Calla as she drew up a chair beside him, holding a bowl of steaming broth she had ladled from a pot bubbling over the coals. Ephraim helped Trevannon to maneuver onto his side and propped up his head with a rolled blanket—apparently the Canaanites permitted no luxury of pillows—and Calla spooned the broth into Trevannon's mouth.

He gulped the first spoonful, said impatiently, "Who was it?"

"Sheriff Vandermeer. Before we made out his identity, I knew we must hide you somehow. I was in a quandary. Calla had the solution. We had a couple of minutes, time enough to lift you off the bunk and slide you onto the floor beneath it. A tight squeeze, but we got you in place, spread a blanket over the cot to hang down and conceal you . . ."

Calla said, bringing the spoon back to his lips, "Then we had Grandmother lie down on the bunk. Nothing could have looked more completely innocent."

"That too was Calla's idea," Ephraim observed wryly. "I must own that I was quite shaken, even paralyzed, by this emergency. And I am far too simple a man to follow such devious female thinking." Calla smiled at the fond chiding in his tone. "Even then, I knew some bad moments in what followed. We'd barely gotten the articles of treatment out of sight and settled ourselves about the table with cups of coffee and expressions of casual innocence when the sheriff came barging through yonder doorway like a winter storm.

"He was not his usual placid self—that was at once obvious. We understood when he told his mission . . . of the boy he insisted that you had shot. I was terribly shocked, of course, and then he asked about you." Ephraim frowned sidelong at his daughter-in-law, his fingers gingerly kneading his right knee. "At which point, Calla kicked me—hard."

Calla said serenely, "Grandpa, I didn't want you to say the wrong thing, before you thought."

"The sheriff is a man I highly respect," Ephraim admitted. "Perhaps, had I followed my first impulse, I would have answered with the truth." He sighed. "Bearing false witness, even in the name of justice, isn't a sin that sits lightly afterward."

Trevannon almost smiled, knowing that Ephraim's scant respect for organized law, his pride in his ability to read a man's character, would have influenced his decision. Still, it was Calla whose response had reflected an absolute and unquestioning trust in him; he met her calm gray gaze now with a sense of humble gratitude that awed him. He knew in that moment that this woman would stand first in his thoughts if he lived to a hundred. And this with the knowledge that all along he'd have expected no less from her; he had instinctively headed here with that fact central to his thoughts.

Ephraim said with a faint embarrassment, as though he'd read Trevannon's mind, "To make the story short, I lied like a trooper. I didn't doubt the sheriff's word, but I felt that he'd been somehow misled. As we talked, the details were clarified. My friend Vandermeer granted that certain things puzzled him . . . though he was certain that you could give the answers. Then he asked about the fire on yonder ridge, which I sheepishly informed him we'd started by accident. He sternly reminded me that it had been mostly a dry year, to take more care—and then, speaking of fires, he said the main house of Kaysee ranch had mysteriously caught fire last night . . . burned to the ground."

Trevannon started to jerk upright; with the stab of pain he sank back. Ephraim shook his head sadly to the unspoken query. "Apparently Kilrain Carter's wife and her mother— burned to death. Terrible," he murmured, still wagging his head. "The sheriff had ridden by on his way here. The Kaysee hands had half killed themselves trying to stop it. Hopeless. And none knew how it had started."

God, she went that far, Trevannon thought, stunned. *That far*. . . . "Vandermeer—he left?"

"He went outside, poked about in some sheds a bit. Was evidently satisfied. Gave me a good-day, and rode off. However, I was cautious enough to drift about the fields telling the men to work as though nothing had happened, to betray nothing out of the ordinary. It was well that I did. . . . An hour ago I chanced to look up at the ridge above the Bench—saw sunlight flash off something. I would hazard that the sheriff is up there with an eagle eye— and field glasses—peeled. He evidently believes that we might have concealed you anywhere in the settlement, that the lot of us would conspire to protect you—and that a lone man searching would be baffled. So he's watching for the smallest betraying move on our parts." Ephraim shook his head sorrowfully. "Always, this man took his duty coldly, as a matter of course . . . now, there is a terrible and savage determination in him. He will leave no stone unturned."

"He still up there?"

"I can't say. We must simply continue as we have. And now, my friend, I have spoken my piece . . . what of yours?"

Trevannon tried to keep it brief, but it seemed a long time before he'd told everything. It involved digging far into the past he'd wanted to forget. He was sweating, his voice weak, when he finished.

"Cassius McQuayle," Ephraim murmured. "How I misjudged that man. Yet—judge not—"

"Grandpa," Calla said with deep concern, "don't trouble him now. Let him rest."

Ephraim set his hands on his knees to rise, but Trevannon detained him, clamping a hand on his arm. "Sir, I got to know."

"It's been a long road for you, Wesley Trevannon," old Waybeck said with great gentleness. "One paved with good and bad. More good, I know, than bad. I know too that whatever solution you choose will be yours alone, for that is your way. I will say this: you have reached a forking in the road; you have a grave decision to make. But you know that. Until you decide—we'll shelter and hide you here, if we have to outwit the very devil."

Calla laughed softly, affectionately. "My devious ways . . . Grandpa, I've corrupted you."

Ephraim settled a gentle hand on her shoulder as he stood. "That—never, my dear. And now we'll eat."

Trevannon lay quietly, the muted drone of Ephraim's midday grace touching only the surface of his mind. What had the old man meant? That he must choose whether to run, or to placidly turn himself over to the law? Likely enough. *That last is his way,* Trevannon thought grimly. *Not mine, and not against a stacked deck.* It would be a murder charge now.

But why should anyone shoot Job Bell? He ran his mind back over the night's events. He'd left the unconscious deputy covered with the cot blanket. The killer had probably made his move before the deputy revived, had fired through the cell door or the barred window without getting a close look at the covered form. The bullet had been intended for him, Trevannon. McQuayle had the motive . . . to wipe out Trevannon's knowledge of his plan to put grabs on that gold-bearing land.

Trevannon exhaled slowly; it was a bitter sigh. Try to prove any of this . . . impossible. No way to escape hanging but to run—and with a wound that would lay him low for several days. Even a slight movement tided rhythmic strokes of pain and dizziness through his body. A black bitterness seethed in him. Everything he'd tried to do since hitting this valley had been selflessly done in the best interests of others. He'd netted this for his pains: helplessly waiting for an angry, deadly-dogged lawman to take him off to jail, a guilty verdict, a hangman's noose.

And yet, he reminded himself, Ephraim and his people were unhesitatingly risking a great deal to help him. This fact beaconed strongly among his dark thoughts. You had to believe in human goodness when you saw its evidence with your own eyes, and there wasn't much finer under the sun.

Young Jerry, gulping down a last mouthful, asked to be excused from the table, and ran over to the bunk. Wes met his large gray eyes in surprise, eyes so like his mother's in their grave frankness . . . for the boy had been painfully shy till now.

Jerry touched a fascinated finger to the butt of the heavy Colt, slung by its shellbelt over the back of a chair by the bunk. "That—that's a nice gun, mister. . . ."

"Like to see it?" Trevannon reached out, lifted the gun from holster.

"Jerry!" Ephraim thundered. "Go outside."

"I was about to take out the shells," Trevannon said dryly.

"No matter; the boy will handle no gun beneath my roof."

"A tool, Mr. Waybeck. Like your hoe. You watch the man behind it."

Old Ephraim's bearded lips became a tight line. "There are some things, sir, on which you and I will never see eye to eye." He clamped on his black hat and tramped outside, his lofty back stiff.

Calla paused in the act of clearing away the dishes, and came over to slap Jerry lightly on the rear. "Go help Grandpa. Go along, now."

The boy edged reluctantly from the room, and Calla sat down by the bunk, her work-strong hands clasped in her lap.

Wes growled, "You like letting him raise that kid on a cloud?"

Calla said quietly, "I know. Jerry is at the age where you can't draw a line between boy and man. He should start to know what life is. But as Grandpa said—this *is* his roof."

Trevannon was silent a moment, said then awkwardly, "I haven't thanked you."

She colored faintly, avoiding his eyes to study a pleat in her skirt. "I just—believed in you. Don't ask me why; I can't—"

"You and me," Wes interrupted quietly, "we're too old for pretendin' games."

"There is no sense to this," she said in a voice grave and

low, and then bit her lip to hide a smile. "Two people don't just . . ."

Trevannon grinned a little. "They do, though. Sometimes, anyway. Since we talked the other day. Only it took me a time to catch up with myself. I don't guess feelings are things you can sort out too neat. We both done our share of mourning . . . life goes on. I can't say this very well."

"You do well enough." Her fingers closed over his, tightly.

For a moment they only sat, a sense of wonder and strangeness still holding them. Then he said, low-voiced, "This isn't much good. We can't—"

He broke off, at once alert, as Ephraim came back through the doorway. "The sheriff is returning," he announced quietly. "He must have become impatient with only waiting. He is coming fast. We'll have to—"

"No hiding," Trevannon said with flat finality. He fought up on his elbows.

Calla gasped. "No, Wes . . ."

He picked up the gun which he'd laid on the blanket, its well-worn cedar grips a hard assurance against his palm. "Help me to the window."

"In that," Ephraim said sternly, "I will not oblige you. Let us help—or give yourself up. In either case—put away your weapon."

Trevannon's grin was a mere tightening of lips. "As you're so fond of remindin' a man, sir—my way is my own. Keep out of it, then." He looked a hard question at Calla.

Without hesitation she bent, got both hands beneath his good shoulder, helped him swing his legs to the floor.

"Calla," Ephraim murmured sadly, "you must know this is wrong. His way is—"

"Mine," she said, "mine, now," and did not look at the old man. She caught Trevannon's full weight on her shoulder as he clumsily stood. For a moment they swayed off-balance. Then with Calla's help he took faltering steps to the single front window. Waves of nausea and pain laid a punishing rhythm through him as she left him leaning against the wall. She brought the chair and he settled heavily onto it. The gun butt was sweat-slick; his hands shook. He ground down hard on his weakness. A greased cloth covered the window opening in lieu of glass, admitting a yellow-murked light. Wes tore it away and laid his gun barrel across the sill.

Vandermeer was very near, riding hard past the first ramshackle dwellings. Trevannon filled his lungs, let out a broken shout: *"That's near enough, Sheriff!"*

Vandermeer saw him and heard him . . . and kept coming. He brought his mount to a skidding halt in the dusty road by Waybeck's yard, swung heavily down. He threw the reins and stood spread-legged, his massive chest rising and falling with hard breathing. Otherwise he looked composed. But his eyes were the glacial calm of chipped ice, his voice bland as iron. "Shoot, you killer, and be damned!"

He drew and cocked his pistol in an unbroken motion.

Yet neither man fired. Across the few yards of dirt that separated them tension strained like a fine drawn thread. For an instant a baffled strangeness filled Vandermeer's broad face. He shook his head doggedly and and came across the yard at a hard trot.

Trevannon sank back into the chair, the hand with the gun dropping limply on his thigh. Resignedly he shut his eyes. *That was it, your decision.*

His eyes shot open, startled by the sudden tug on his hand. His gun was gone. Calla held it double-handed, thumbs dragging back the hammer. She wheeled at the same time, running to put her back against the wall opposite the door. She raised the heavy Colt's at arm's length, pointing it at the door. Old Mrs. Waybeck let out a high, tremulous wail.

"No, Calla, no," Trevannon heard himself say—and

then Vandermeer reached the door. A powerful kick sent it swinging inward. The sheriff lunged into the room, stopping his headlong rush even as he pivoted on a heel, his pistol swinging to cover Trevannon. He halted in mid-motion, only then seeing Calla with the gun leveled at his chest.

CHAPTER 17

"YOUNG WOMAN," JANS VANDERMEER SAID STOLIDLY, "IF you mean to use that—do so now."

Calla stood tall and stiff, her eyes flashing. She lowered the gun very slowly; when it touched her skirt, she let up the hammer gently, let the gun clatter to the floor.

Vandermeer scooped it up and rammed it in his belt, motioned curtly at Trevannon with his own weapon.

"Get up."

Old Ephraim moved foward, lifting a restraining hand. "Wait, friend Jans. The man is hurt. And there are several things you must hear."

Vandermeer's glacial attention shifted to the old man. "I think you have said enough. You lied to me to shield a murderer. Of all men I know, I had not thought this of you. Shall I listen more to a man who baldly breaches faith?"

"My good friend," Ephraim chided gently, "would I lie to save a man I *believed* was a murderer? Would I?"

Vandermeer scowled. "I had not thought this of you," he repeated. "You lied for this man once; why not again? I am sorry. This thing will go hard for you, Ephraim, and for your family."

"At least listen—"

"I am not disposed to listen where *this* is concerned," Vandermeer said harshly. He made a sweeping motion of his hand toward Trevannon. "The signs were plain. My deputy had been struck over the head before he was shot . . .

hard enough to lay him low for hours. To escape, it was not necessary to then put a bullet in him with his own gun." He tapped the butt of Job's weapon in his belt. "Yet this man did so in cold blood."

"Wasn't that gun that did the job, Sheriff," Trevannon whispered.

"You will prove this."

Trevannon slumped against the chairback, rubbing his head between his hands. Fever pulsed hotly behind his temples. He felt weary and sick and disgusted. He could not prove it, not with that gun recently fired and the expended shell still chambered. The bullet that had brought down Tige Menefee. There were other facts, of course . . . Tige's body, his own wounding by Tige. But this bullheaded lawman would not listen now, and he was too dizzy and tired to explain any more. He summoned strength to his voice. "I'm ready, Sheriff. Let's go."

"No, Wes," Calla began, starting toward him. "You can't ride—"

Trevannon lifted a hand sharply to cut her off. A horseman was coming up the road at a hard gallop. He leaned toward the window, winced and bit down on his lip. Leaned his head in his hands and waited for the surge of agony to recede. "Who is it?" he whispered.

He heard Calla's light steps move to the window. "It's that Treat . . . Bill Treat."

He raised his head and stared at her. Heard the slobber of racking breaths from a hard-driven horse, the broken shuffle of its halting. Then Treat's gruff tones, holding a rough note of friendliness. "Howdy, kid. Your Grandpa in?"

Trevannon gritted his teeth and heaved his weight forward. Caught the windowsill and gripped it hard. Treat was standing by his horse, his clothes dusty and sweat-patched. His face was red and shining beneath the shadow of his hatbrim, looking down at young Jerry, who'd evidently been coming back from a neighbor's when Treat had accosted him. Treat glanced up quickly now; his gaze locked with Trevannon's. *What the hell brings him here?* Wes wondered.

Treat's hard grin parted his lips; he dropped a thick hand to the boy's towhead. "Let's go in and see him, eh, bucko?" He came on across the yard, propelling the boy ahead with a heavy hand between his shoulders.

The door was ajar, and it creaked thinly as he pushed it wide, commanding a full view of the room. He halted on the threshold, hand settled loosely on the boy's thin shoulder. He grinned widely, but Trevannon saw the wild glints race through his milky stare.

"Howdy, Dutchy. Folks. Trevannon . . ."

"Bill," the sheriff said urgently, "Bill, you have word of Job?"

"Man, he's good and dead by now." Treat's right arm was held close to his body, his hand hidden by the boy, and now it came up holding his leveled Remington .44 above Jerry's shoulder. His left forearm shifted, locking brutally around the boy's throat and pulling him tightly against Treat's legs.

"Bill!" Vandermeer choked. "What is this?"

"You'd have found out," Treat smiled. "That's why you'll never know. Better drop them guns. One in your hand's pointed the wrong way, and I got a dead bead on you. Big man like yourself might last long enough to get a bullet in me . . . but I wouldn't try. Not with the boy in line."

Vandermeer's empty hand formed a fist at his side. "I would make a guess, Bill. You shot Job. I thought I saw fear in you, there in the doctor's office. But I could not guess why. Why, then?"

"Dutchy. The boy." Treat said it confidently.

With a hard-wrenched sigh Vandermeer let his gun fall. He lifted the other weapon from his belt and dropped it; it bounced at an angle and skidded across the floor.

Now Treat moved deeper into the room, holding the boy in front of him. "Over against the wall by Trevannon. All of you." Vandermeer obeyed phlegmatically, tramping over to stand by Trevannon's chair. Ephraim Waybeck followed more slowly. Calla was breathing deeply and steadily, her body tense.

"You too, missus. Your boy won't be hurt, 'less one of you moves wrong. Trevannon there, and Dutchy . . . they're my meat."

Calla stepped to Ephraim's side, and the old man took her hand, murmuring, "Be steady now. Be strong."

Treat's irritable glance slid toward Ephraim's wife. "You. Old woman. You don't hear good?"

Mrs. Waybeck was rocking gently in her chair, fixedly watching Treat's gun. Her eyes were vacant, her lips moving. ". . . . *And behold, a pale horse: and he that sat on him, his name was Death; and Hades followed with him. . . .*"

Treat wiped a hand quickly across his mouth, his first betrayal of uneasy tenseness. "What's the matter with her?"

"You ought to know, Mr. Treat," Calla spoke softly. "You did this to her, you and your riders. It must be a relief to forget so easily."

"What'n hell are you talking about?"

"Her son. The man I married. This boy's father. He was killed when you raided our homestead that night, six months ago."

Treat grunted. "Hell, I ain't forgot. Was me that shot that fella. We had orders from Carter to just shoot high and scare you. Me, I figured to serve your sort a sharper lesson . . . pinked your husband square when he tried to drag a Kaysee man off his hoss. Everybody figured a chance slug got to him." Treat wagged his head with mock sorrow. "They was all regretful."

Old Ephraim made a sound deep in his chest and took a step. "No," Calla whispered, holding his arm with all her strength. Slowly the old man stepped back, his stare burning on Treat.

"That's smart, missus," Treat said. "Do beat all what it takes to kill some critters. Trevannon there, he looks half dead awready. Someone use you for a target?"

"Someone," Trevannon said quietly.

"Be a shame to end it so fast then. All right, Dutchy. You stand nice and still—wouldn't want the wrong one gettin' hit. . . ."

Wes dropped weakly in his chair, his head bowed on his chest. His breathing was a strained rasp, telling of helpless weakness. And so Treat contemptuously ignored him, fixing his decision first on Jans Vandermeer. Trevannon's eyes had already flicked sidelong, marking the distance to Job's gun which, when the sheriff dropped it, had bounded to within a few feet of the wall. It lay in a dust-hazed sunshaft a yard from Ephraim's boots.

The move had to be his; Treat had already discounted him, but was wary of the others. Did he have the strength left, the speed? He would have to dive for the floor, endangering Ephraim and Calla who would be standing directly behind him. And Jerry. The crown of the boy's head just reached Treat's breastbone.

Aim high, Trevannon thought, *and careful, for God's sake* . . . and then there was no time to think more, for Treat was raising the Remington to arm's length, sighting carefully down on Vandermeer's broad chest.

Trevannon was sitting sideways, his knees bent, his toes firm against the clay floor. With a mighty effort he straightened his legs and launched his body hard and low, his shoulder powering into Vandermeer's hip. The impact drove the sheriff piling into Ephraim and Calla, as Treat's gun bellowed deafeningly in the room. Trevannon twisted his shoulder upward as it struck the sheriff so that it slid off without slowing his sideward lunge, and he rolled as he fell. He hit the floor at the others' feet, squarely on his back, his left hand flinging out with straining haste for Job's gun even as the painful impact smashed through his body. It was a blind reach, but his hand closed true over the butt; and thumbed the hammer as he brought the gun up.

Though it happened in the space of a quick breath, he had the agonizing sense that he was moving with a trancelike deliberation. Though he didn't remember that till afterward.

His maneuver might yet have failed if Jerry hadn't suddenly writhed and kicked in Treat's grasp. The boy had stood quietly till now, only moving when he saw Trevannon move. Treat had his hands full. He made the mistake of trying to hold the kid, and then, with a curse, flung him aside and aimed quickly down at Trevannon.

The Colt arced around at the end of Trevannon's extended arm, and he saw the ruddy patch of Treat's face blur beyond the sights, and then he shot. Treat's heavy shape was dissolving toward the floor before his gun went off by reflex.

Blinded by powder fumes, Trevannon shrank instinctively against the floor as Treat's shot roared deafeningly between the confining walls. Then he saw Treat sprawled with one arm flung out, the other bent and pillowing his head. Wes tried to raise himself on a hand, grunted in pain and slipped back. The room swam; black shadows rocked in his vision.

Then Calla's strong arms went around him, and with Ephraim's assistance she got him to the bunk. She was already loosening his blood-soaked bandages as Vandermeer bent down by Treat and turned his head.

Not wanting to see, Trevannon looked as Vandermeer curtly asked Ephraim for something to cover the body. The old man was speaking quietly to his wife, and when her soft moaning had ceased, he tramped from the room, taking the boy with him. Trevannon watched Calla's face, the shadings of concerned emotions that colored its still calm as she removed the last of the bandages and began to clean his wound.

He set his teeth and bore the pain through a silence that held, unbroken by Vandermeer who stood stolidly by, his arms folded, his eyes chill as a winter sky. Ephraim returned with a piece of ragged tarp. A minute later, he and the sheriff bore it from the room, hammocked around the dead weight of Treat.

Trevannon closed his eyes. This time there was no way out. Coming to grips with this fact had smothered his last spark of resistance. He couldn't have run had he wished to; to this he was fatalistically resigned.

Vandermeer returned shortly and indicated his wish to hear the whole thing from the beginning. Trevannon tried to speak, but Calla hushed him and with impassioned defiance told Wes's story. Vandermeer's few spare, cold-eyed comments were merely questions.

When she'd concluded, Calla observed acidly, "You'll be wanting to take the man who saved your life on to prison now, I've no doubt—though the trip will certainly kill him."

"I am not in such a hurry," Vandermeer observed with ponderous gravity. "Neither do I want to risk his escaping again. I have no haste for another lengthy chase. First, Ephraim, I wish you to take me to the burned hill yonder where you say Tige Menefee's body is. I wish to see if that happened as you said—"

"Certainly," gibed Calla. "We wouldn't expect you to take our word."

"Calla," Ephraim said wearily, and to the sheriff, with a nod: "I will do that."

"I will also ask for the loan of a wagon to take the bodies of Treat and Menefee back to Kaysee. I think there will be no need for a coroner's investigation. Tomorrow I return, and then wait till you are well enough to be moved."

Trevannon stared at him, this man of iron, wondering if the brain behind that stolid face ever knew a subtle flicker of indecision, of uncertainty, as to its course. "You're too damned kind."

Vandermeer grunted without even a twitch of his lips. "I give you thanks. That for saving my life. What more does a breaker of laws expect—"

"From you? Nothing. Not a damned thing. Don't lose any sleep."

"From a man dedicated to keeping the law," Vandermeer went on imperturbably. And, with a touch of unexpected irony: "I am thankful for your understanding."

He pivoted and walked from the room. Shortly Trevannon heard the sheriff hooraw a team into motion as he and Ephraim rode out. He looked at Calla and tried to speak, but her fingers touched his mouth and her lips formed, "Rest."

Gratefully he closed his eyes. And slept. A restless, nightmarish sleep, and when he awoke with a start, he was feverish and bathed in sweat. It was hours later, and the windows were dark. The lamp on the table flickered a sallow glow, picking out the mounded shaped of Ephraim and his wife in their bunks, the quiet, deep breathing of the boy in the bunk above Trevannon.

Calla's back was toward him, and she was hanging a blanket to a pair of nails in the rafters by a far wall where she'd improvised a pallet of straw for her own bed. She slipped behind the screening blanket, and he heard the sliding whisper of cloth. He knew a lonely man's foolish embarrassment at the intimate sounds of her undressing, and then the sensation ebbed quickly. There should not be, could never be, a withholding, a false reticence, where she was concerned. The feeling had grown between them till it was as strong and certain as Calla herself . . . and, he thought bleakly, ended before it had begun.

She stepped out wearing a long gray nightgown, and moved to the table to turn up the lamp, afterward coming across to his bunk. Briefly her body cut sideways between his vision and the light, and the glow diffused through the gown to profile the sturdy fullness of breasts and hips and thighs beneath its loose folds. Above his weakness and sickness, he felt the quick stir of his blood. She bent at his side, the pale rope of her unbound hair crumpling softly on his shoulder. She felt his forehead, and his hand went out and caught hers.

"Oh . . . Wes, you're awake."

His hands on her shoulders guided her firm weight down against him, and her lips were full and giving. It was a moment of urgent hunger that was a desperate protest against the injustice, the hopelessness, of their situation. The shattering pain of his wound jarred him back to sanity;

with his recoiling wince, Calla drew back, her breathing
deep and ragged.

"Nothing," she whispered hopelessly. "We'll be apart
soon . . . and we can't even have the time that's left."

Wes drew her face to his and stroked her head, talking
quietly. Giving her a comfort he didn't feel, with tomorrow
laying its bleak certainty across his thoughts.

CHAPTER 18

TREVANNON SLEPT FITFULLY, THEN MORE SOUNDLY AS HIS fever cooled, and when he awoke late the following morning he felt better, even refreshed. Calla was preparing the noon meal, busily stirring about the kitchen as she had been the first day he'd come here. From the yard echoed the bite of Ephraim's ax as he tussled with a stubborn chunk of cordwood, and the old woman creaked to and fro in her rocking chair, her gnarled fingers moving over the pages of her Bible.

But now there was something automatic and unreal in the workaday bustle, and the bright-blocked sunlight that fell on his blankets held a brittle and cheerless warmth.

Young Jerry moped in the doorway, and he was the first to see Trevannon awake. He came to the bunk, saying gravely, "Are you going away?"

Calla turned, brushing a strand of hair from her eyes. She made a movement as though to shoo the boy away, but Trevannon's eyes met hers in a wordless communion so natural he knew a painful irony in it, and he shook his head.

He ruffled the boy's hair. "Not for a while, anyway."

Jerry's eyes were very direct and sober. "You don't have to, ever. We can hide you. I know a cave over by the hills. Like Jesse James and all them have. Specky Burdick and me play outlaw and Injuns over there."

Calla remarked with only faint censure, "What did Grandfather tell you about that?"

"Said he'd whup both of us if we played at shooting people again. Even tol' Specky's pa to keep us apart so's we'd stay out of mischief."

"Well, then."

"Aw, Ma."

"So long as we live with Grandpa, we must do as he says."

"Sure, I know . . . but Mr. Trevannon don't. Do you?"

"No," Trevannon said slowly. "Only there's a thing you got to understand. When you stop taking orders from other folks, you got to start taking them from yourself."

Jerry considered this carefully, then said, "I don't get that."

"Well . . ." Trevannon eased himself up on an elbow, frowning gently. "Grown folks don't have to take orders from anyone if they've a mind not to. But that don't mean they can step on other folks' feet when they feel like it."

"Sure, everyone knows that."

"That's why there's rules they make to keep each other in line. Everyone knows the rules—laws—and mostly they keep them. When they don't, other people have to see they do."

"Like that old sheriff," Jerry nodded, and then: "Did you break a law?"

"I took money that other people earned. I thought I was put on sore enough to justify it. I did some other wrong things too, which came first. You do wrong things long enough, you start telling yourself they're right. Pretty soon you're breaking a lot of rules and a lot of people get hurt. That's why the rules got to be kept—even when you can't help thinking they're wrong. Understand me?"

Jerry nodded, but a little sulkily, and then he burst out, "But if you *know* you done bad and you're sorry, you don't do wrong again, do you?"

"Some do. I'd say no, though."

"Then you don't have to let that sheriff take you away," he pointed out triumphantly.

Trevannon was mustering his thoughts for his own benefit as much as the boy's, and he wondered wryly whether he would have sounded so self-righteous if he were unhurt now, capable of escape. Still, a man made his road rocky with his own mistakes; the boy had to see that. "A man has to pay up, Jerry. You see—"

He broke off at the sound of a wagon coming, and then he heard Vandermeer's phlegmatic greeting, Ephraim's cold reply. In a moment, the sheriff's formidable bulk filled the doorway. He sank onto the chair by Trevannon's bunk, elbows on knees, his big hands laced together, and quietly spoke.

Vandermeer's contained calm had returned. Trevannon learned why: Job Bell would live. Cassius McQuayle had been found dead in his office, apparently of a heart attack. Bill Treat had been seen by several citizens leaving McQuayle's office on the run, then riding from town at a furious pace. Vandermeer had concluded that McQuayle and Treat had thrown in together to carry through McQuayle's scheme to get the gold-bearing tract. Treat's part was to kill Trevannon before he let out word of the gold. This explanation made sense, at least . . . and McQuayle's heart had given out when he'd learned that Job Bell had named Treat as the would-be killer, which would include McQuayle as accomplice . . . or he and Treat had quarreled. The details were not important, and Jans Vandermeer had other matters weighing his mind.

Concerning the burning of the Kaysee main house, he said, an unexpected development had come to light. Yesterday afternoon, when Vandermeer was returning with the wagon containing the bodies of Treat and Menefee, he'd followed the relatively level slopes of the creek bottomlands. In a wide, deep pond which broke the onrushing

stream at a low point, he had found the body of Andrea
Carter floating face down. Evidently Mrs. Carter had
herself fired the house, then had ridden to this pool and
drowned herself. . . .

Vandermeer had taken the three bodies to Kaysee, where
he'd consulted with Gabe Morrow. Gabe had given it as his
opinion that Mrs. Carter's actions were precipitated by grief
for her late husband. Trevannon silently guessed that old
Gabe had shrewdly sized up the real truth, but would never
speculate aloud on it. And that was best, Trevannon
thought . . . best that this strange tormented girl's secret
die with her. Even the sad pity he now felt belonged to
memory. It was as though the few days he'd spent at Kaysee
had been lived in another world, and he no longer cared
about the ranch or its ultimate fate. There was here and now,
and there was Calla—yes, and the boy. He had to give the
future a realistic eye; if there was even a chance. . . .

"Sheriff—I shot a clerk on that holdup. I reckoned he
wasn't much hurt, but I wonder if you know—"

"When I returned to Coldbrook last night, I found a man
from Cedar Wells waiting. Sent by my wife to get word of
me. Among other things, he said the young clerk is already
back on the job." The sheriff paused, weighing his next
words. "I told him I was still working on the holdup. That
is all I have told anyone, except Gabe Morrow—yet."

With puzzled alertness, yet not daring to hope, Trevannon said slowly, "You stalling, Sheriff?"

Vandermeer rose brusquely, restlessly paced a circle.
Then he faced him, growling, "Damn it all. Damn you,
Trevannon. It is a hell of a debt for a lawman to owe a
bankrobber."

"Sorry," Trevannon said patiently, and waited.

"You are sorry!" Vandermeer snorted explosively. "Is a
man to forget so easily that you saved his life?"

"Try harder," Trevannon advised him coldly.

Vandermeer dropped his bristling front and sank onto the

chair. He stirred a great paw in an aimless, weary gesture. "That is not what I mean. You understand? I am a man of law; this comes first. It is myself who angers me. My very father I could bring to justice if the matter demanded."

"Sounds more like you, Sheriff."

Vandermeer's merciless gaze seemed to probe the root nature of the man on the bunk. "So. You think you know much. Well, you are not a fool. And maybe, if you had come as an orphan to a strange country, when you have nothing, when you look for something . . . if you had studied long to master a strange language and had found with relief a thing in which to believe . . . a system of laws which promises justice for all men and punishment for those who laugh at justice . . . if you spend days and nights struggling with great books to find the heart and meaning of this thing called law, this thing to which you have dedicated yourself. . . . Maybe, Mr. Trevannon, when you have done all this which sounds so easy in the saying, then you will know what I have tried to learn."

He scowled, looked down at his hands and massaged them, scowling slightly. Trevannon was faintly embarrassed, that this iron man was trying with difficulty to express the creed which centered his life.

Vandermeer continued slowly, "I live by the law, but I see it in my own terms. It must be a human thing, for it was made for humans. So. Ephraim Waybeck is my great friend. And this sharp-tongued lady," he motioned toward Calla, "is a fine woman. They know right and wrong well. It is not the law they fight, but a thing they think is wrong. But the law should always do right, eh? So I see it . . . justice wears a blindfold, but justice must not be blind. Punishment is to balance wrong, to prevent more wrong. Now . . . a man has suffered for wrong. He has tried to atone. Even when he could have watched the man of law who has come to take him shot down, he throws himself across the way of a bullet to save that man."

Trevannon raised himself on his elbows, frowning. "Don't get me wrong—"

"I do not; that is my point," the Dutchman said sternly. "And do not interrupt, please. Punishment is for a reason. When this reason is gone, there must be an end of punishment. Otherwise there is not justice." He set his hands on his knees and rose with ponderous gravity, his frosty eyes meeting Trevannon's with decision. A decision hadn't been easy, but once made, it was set in this iron-principled man's stubborn mind with the weighted certainty of a giant ridgepole timber lowered into place. "You are a man who has learned his own worth by a bitter road. Now live by that worth."

Phlegmatically he clamped on his hat and walked with his stolid, sweeping stride from the room. Trevannon lay unmoving, listening to the creak of leather as the sheriff mounted his horse, hearing his gruff farewell to Ephraim, the dying away of brisk hoofbeats. Jans Vandermeer was riding off, turning his back on the fugitive he had grimly bloodhounded. The money would be returned to its bank, accompanied by a small lie that reflected a bigger truth as this strange man of law saw it. . . .

Ephraim Waybeck came to the doorway, his seamed and bearded face alight, and he looked on them all and was wordless. Calla came to Trevannon and he held her hand tightly. For the moment there was nothing to say.

The old woman gave a little murmuring sound and then she stood and made her slow, groping way to the bunk. Her trembling fingers went out and traced lightly over Trevannon's brow. A little smile touched her soundlessly moving lips as she glided slowly back to her chair.

"She understands something of all that's happened," Calla said softly. "She was trying to tell you that. Perhaps she may even recover now. We've wanted that so much. This could be a beginning."

The boy scrambled to his feet and ran over to stand between them, leaning on his mother's arm where it reached to touch Trevannon's. His gray eyes were serious and hopeful. "Is Mr. Trevannon staying, Ma?"

Trevannon had not heard Calla's laugh before, and now it brimmed with her quiet strength. "Yes, Mr. Trevannon will stay now."

Tales of the West by T.V. OLSEN

By the year 2000, 2 out of 3 Americans could be illiterate.

It's true.

Today, 75 million adults...about one American in three, can't read adequately. And by the year 2000, U.S. News & World Report envisions an America with a literacy rate of only 30%.

Before that America comes to be, you can stop it...by joining the fight against illiteracy today.

Call the Coalition for Literacy at toll-free **1-800-228-8813** and volunteer.

**Volunteer
Against Illiteracy.
The only degree you need
is a degree of caring.**

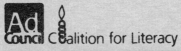

Ad Council Coalition for Literacy

LV-2